Escape To

Butterfly Ave

Escape To Butterfly Ave

HIP HOP NOVEL

MAX EVANS

URBAN CONTEMPORARIES
PRIMARY BOOKS
LONG BEACH, CALIFORNIA

SOCIAL MEDIA:

LONG BEACH WRITER

Dedicated to the LBC

Escape to Butterfly Ave
First Edition
2022
Copyright © 2022 Max Evans
979-8-82-716552-1

REMIX FICTION

Remix Fiction is a subgenre of literature that reimagines stories discovered in songs. In this book, Hip Hop cuts adapted as chapters blend seamlessly into the narrative structure of a novel. Therefore, chapter transitions replicate DJ changeovers, aptly termed *scratch-sitions*.

Table of Cuts

*On and on and on and on—*Yo!
Freestyle flow to make the crowd just go.
The old to the new . . . the new to the old.

—Doug E. Fresh

SHOEBOX FEVER

. . . and on and on and on and on the day before the Covid lockdown began, I remember picking up an order at a restaurant for a delivery service when these old heads got loud in the line.

"Kids these days," one complained. "They don't know nothing about keeping it real."

"How can they keep it real?" the other said. "All they do is play on their phones. Take pictures of pizza."

Half a year later, on Día de los Muertos, I wish those old guys were inside my apartment now. I'd rise up off this futon—where I've been nursing a hangover—and sit their asses down.

I'd be like, "You wanna keep it real? Cool, then. I'll keep it real with you. Because my weekend was real—realer than the realest real can get."

Out of everything that happened the last few days, where would I even start? Maybe I would begin by telling them about the cops slapping on the cuffs . . . or skateboarding through the city holding my infant . . . can't forget the fight with my crackhead neighbor . . . or maybe the heated argument with my ex-fiancé's mom . . . then there was that moment I yacked at the bar.

Speaking of throwing up, that's when all the shit went down. This past Friday, my daughter Shawna cried insanely: teething phase. She had spent the week in my arms, so no money was earned from delivering food, or donating plasma at the center, or mailing inventory from my living room.

My back tightened. I had to put Shawna on the floor. I twisted this way, that way. I folded in half, torso bobbing. Baby girl erupted a volcano of vocal cords and flung the chilled ring from the fridge. Her tiny hands squeezed the air, demanding to be picked up.

Before I gave, I needed a minute.

Request denied—her mouth hinged wider. In the middle of her red licorice gums, the puffy membrane was engorged with puss. A thin film showed a race between her bottom teeth, both growing in crooked like my dad's.

Earlier this week, I had joked with the ER doctor that nail clippers could pop that bubble.

"No," she scolded, her N95 mask bumping into her face shield. "You must not do that."

"Alright."

"Please, listen."

"No problem."

"Everything will be fine."

"Yup."

"You must let nature take its course."

Swear to God, that lady would not let it go. She explained with a pitched tone what I already knew—infections, botched jobs, child abuse reports. Nurses come at me with the same *wah-wah* voice. They sound as if they're giving instructions to a five-year-old.

Okay, I get it. You have a young dad with tatted arms in your office. But don't act like my daughter isn't with me half the time. And don't treat me like I wasn't there for her first breath, first step.

By the way, your clinic walls are thinner than wipees. I hear you explain options to the mothers (some, who never passed junior high) with your everyday voice. And I've read every pamphlet in the lobby, including "How to Talk with Baby." But you need a brochure to comprehend that talking at *Da-da* with a *wah-wah* tone is a *nuh-uh-uh*.

My mouth remained shut while she rambled about scratch mittens. Never would I nuke her baby bottle, either.

"Listen, Miss," I wanted to say. "Just because my nips don't pump milk does not mean I'm clueless with my daughter. Just like you, a cell phone fits in my pocket, and I've memorized the three most important letters in the alphabet: *www*."

Baby girl continued her screech at my feet Friday night. The frequency guaranteed a visit from the on-site landlord. I scooped up Miss Wiggle who shimmied in my grasp, mimicking inflatable tube men at car lots.

Bouncing at my knees, I said to her, "It's okay."

Shawna flung around her twenty pounds. My back throbbed from old injuries caused by failing railslides on my skateboard.

"It's okay," I repeated, but more to myself.

I stared out the barred window. Across the alley, the glass condo under construction was quiet. The cranes with lit-up orange flags were meant to alert low-flying aircraft.

"They're the highest the city has ever seen," my dad recently said.

The lifts on the building's exterior resembled cages, ugly cousins to the scaffold walkways. Every completed floor dimmed my natural light and darkened my whole apartment to a shade of cardboard.

Remember the Old Woman Who Lived in a Shoe? Well, I live in a Vans shoebox. My studio is a bottom-floor corridor, long and narrow. The fixtures are random, as if a giant kid late on a design project threw in a bathtub, heater, and cabinets, then squirted in superglue and shook the contents for extra credit.

Upon entry, you can slap the vintage *Thrasher*

calendar hanging on the refrigerator. Without taking another step, you become witness to the world's smallest bathroom. Zoom in lower, a little bit lower, and there's the toilet where all the frozen burritos stacked in the fridge will land. To block the view inside the empty doorframe, a shower curtain hangs from a pull-up bar.

The back of my apartment features half of a fireplace mantle—the owners cemented the part where the logs would go—with the other half stretching into my neighbor's unit. The brick top holds my keys, wallet, and sunglasses. To the side of the mantle, a metal security door opens to the alley. Shawna's diapers help to stabilize our trashcan, and the homeless who open the lid cuss from the stench. Only the closest homies know about the "doo-doo key," my spare taped underneath.

With limited real estate, I carried Shawna across the apartment, from the back door to the front door, the front door to the back door, skirting the futon on each pass. I imagined ollying the flattened cushion and catching air above her diaper bag, the two of us together, rising higher than the commercial jets I'll fly someday.

The only strip of Earth I've cruised more than that matted lane of carpet is the skate park. I spent entire weekends there by the beach, smoking and grinding, even after the sun sloped behind the Rite-

Aid where me and Angela, Shawna's mom, used to kiss. When my ankles would bug, I would lean against the chain link fence, elbows lounging over the top, and smirk at the action.

Like that time a Mastiff wearing a pink bowtie ditched the dog zone, leash dragging, to chase down a squirrel. The massive dog stopped on a dime to nab a kid's penny board and escaped with it down Broadway Avenue. Or, when the lesbian bartender with the septum piercing socked up a new kid for snaking her turn. We tried to warn him, but his ears musta been packed with slide wax. Then there was that time when these out-of-towners claimed to be sponsored even though they couldn't ollie a volleyball. Meanwhile, the resident rider with an eyepatch rode past them juggling Krylon cans. Skillage. And this one never failed—drunk dads. They would climb the ramp, fantasizing about their heydays, only for gravity to smack them back to reality. For those classic fails, we offered a round of golf claps. But the best times were when the pros on tour would show love. They'd pop their trunks and dish out free merch.

More than anything though, I would never forget the day that everyone stopped in their tracks. Not just those of us paying dues to the concrete. I'm saying *everybody* at the park, the bodybuilders knocking dips between benches, the vendors selling candles at the farmers market, the parents filming kids on swings, froze at that moment.

We all full-on heard the same cry. The rapid thrust of sound was not the wail of a human. Closer to a nagging meow. But more powerful than a cat. Everyone searched around, wondering what the hell it was. Traffic rushed past when fingers began pointing toward the street.

The squawk was coming from the shadows. When a claw entered the sun, I low-key thought a turkey was roaming through Long Beach. But then, its curvy neck gleamed a metallic blue, and its purple back shimmied, sprouting a glittery bouquet of olive-shaped eyes. Cell phones popped out to record the wide fan of iridescent feathers ruffling over the sidewalk. From that point on, the street leading to the beach became known as "Peacock Route."

Crazy to think that all happened four years ago. Senior year. My legs used to kill me from those daily grind sessions, yet they were not nearly as fatigued as my arms became from carrying Shawna.

This whole week, by any means possible, I tried to distract my daughter from her discomfort. I played her favorite baby shows. Cruised PCH with the windows down. Watched planes land at the airport. When a 737 taxied the runway, I told Shawna, "One day, Daddy will fly those."

After I own a few skate shops, I'll earn my pilot's license. For now, I work through the pandemic by delivering food and donating plasma. I tested positive for Covid during the summer and scored a place that paid one hundred dollars per draw. Supposedly the antibodies stay in your system for six months. Until mine run dry, I donate twice a week—the maximum times allowed—which gives me a little money to buy skating goods.

Skate shops have been closing left and right, so I purchase products to sell online. Although my inventory is limited, I designed an official looking webpage, maximizing my sales by advertising on social media. My main problem currently: boxes. Boxes are everywhere in my studio. Three big ones filled with quarter pipes double as my coffee table. All this hustle makes collecting unemployment not worth it.

The drive-thru pantries have been a blessing, too. When they ask how many people I live with, I answer "Five" so that they place additional bags on my backseat. Any goods I don't like, or don't have time to cook, I give to my neighbor. You've never seen a bag of onions make someone smile bigger.

But no matter what I had tried to amuse Shawna this week, she lost interest. Her hands opened and closed, opened and closed, her code for, "Lift me! Lift me!"

Typically, my girl was mesmerized by skater documentaries and fell asleep on my lap. But she had been clingy since I picked her up the previous Saturday, and with my patience running low, I had become the Old Woman Who Lived in a Shoe—I didn't know what to do.

My last shot at calming her down Friday afternoon was to visit K, short for Kaleb. Shawna loves his brown chihuahua. But little Chewbacca grew tired of her screeching, so the patient dog punched through the pet door. Zero tail movement.

"Chewbacca," K called. "Get back here."

I knew how it felt to reach that limit.

"Dude," I said. "No worries," and buckled Shawna into my old Cadillac.

K motioned a pint glass to his mouth, confirming the boys wanted to grab drinks the next night.

I turned twenty-two almost a month ago, but Shawna had been with me at that time. The following week, the boys had online college midterms to complete. And then this week, Shawna was with me again. I couldn't wait to celebrate because my twenty-first birthday was canceled since Angela was almost due with Shawna.

After my daughter's birth, I rarely went out, but when I did, the drink tabs were increasing. A major reason was that I gave up weed. Once the paternity test had proven Shawna was mine (Ang was pissed that I asked), I vowed to stop smoking. I loved my herb, and it was accepted and all, but Shawna would begin elementary school in a few years. I would be the youngest parent there, and I refused to be the burnout in a flannel fiending for a toke at orientation. So, before having the chance to slam back shots for both of my birthdays, I would have to sweat another night in the shoebox.

Shawna refused to be put down. Not even for three seconds so Daddy could take a leak. With baby pressed to my chest in the bathroom, I aimed a yellow stream into the toilet, the same toilet where I had flushed my final stash. The seat has been permanently raised since Angela moved back in with her mom, better known as Miss Jackson.

This past summer, my symptoms began with crazy fatigue. I waited hours in my car to be tested. My splitting headache was worsened by worry that my old ride might break down in the line. Before they swiveled that giant Q-tip up my nose, I told Angela—to be on the safe side—to stay at Miss Jackson's until the results came back.

I quarantined for ten days. My isolation period in the shoebox was boring, but it gave me the time to update my webpage and research where to donate my blood. They call it "convalescent" plasma which was fitting since I felt like a convalescent laid up in an old folks' home with no visitors.

The city cleared my health status, but Angela stayed away for a few extra days.

"To be on the safe side," Miss Jackson said.

I consented because Covid had started in the spring and information on the virus changed every day. Sometimes, every hour.

For my girls to have clean things to wear, I sprayed disinfectant on their clothes to pack into a box that once held a shipment of elbow pads. Miss J promised to pick up their stuff with Shawna in the backseat. At the time, since gatherings were banned, the new thing had been for a parade of cars to honk past a house as celebration. But after two weeks apart, all I wanted was to wave to her little face.

I remember feeling good about my choice to wait longer. Not only was I erring on the side of caution before holding my daughter, but I thought a breakthrough moment of trust was being shared with Miss Jackson. In my mind, we were combining forces to protect the ones we loved.

But Miss Jackson treated the clothes pick up like a Grand Prix pitstop. She hit the brakes at my back steps, hopped out with gloves, and jetted down the alley in her Lexus.

"Shawna was taking a nap at home," Miss Jackson said. "I didn't want to wake her."

Little did I know, Miss J had been plotting and scheming the whole time. She drilled into Angela's head to go it alone, complaining I wasn't in school and didn't hold a regular job. She pointed out that Ang and her older sister were raised without their father, and hadn't they come out fine?

Not only did my fiancé undergo a change of heart, but Miss Jackson extended my quarantine from my daughter. That bullshit woulda continued for more than a month if it hadn't been for my dad's former client, a lawyer whom he helped to market a cantina, who intervened on my behalf. It was a rough situation every time I saw Miss Jackson after that, but in order for me to get back with Angela, I needed to win over her mom. I just didn't want Shawna to go through what I had to with my divorced parents. I wanted my daughter to live happily under one roof.

I was mid-stream when Shawna jerked. I sprinkled the toilet rim. The humidity and the state fires were endless this fall, and her head suspended over the porcelain tub. I pressed both hands to her sweaty back, refusing to let her slip. By the time her squirms weakened, my boxers belted across my nutsack, which in turn slanted the elastic band between my balls, squeezing the left one up.

Meanwhile, everything below my knees got hosed. The floor, bathmat, TP tower. While stepping out of my damp bottoms, my foot landed on Shawna's teething ring. Rather than squat, I attempted to pick it up with my toes. Between the coat of pee and the slobber, gripping the orange plastic was difficult. After a few tries, I managed to transfer the ring to my free hand. Her mom woulda boiled off the germs, but I just ran the ring under the sink.

I was about to slide the teether back into

Shawna's mouth, but I found sanitizer to kill off the germs. Still, baby girl wasn't about that life because just as I flushed, she dropped the ring into the toilet.

Dude, I thought. Seriously?

The plastic circle spun.

I zoned out hard and imagined texting Angela: "She won't calm down and shit. Can I bring her over tonight? Better yet, could you come pick her up? My car's messing up again."

But I knew Miss Jackson over her shoulder would say, "See, I told you Alex can't take care of her. Why did you agree to split custody?"

The water level in the toilet rose.

I stood there, half-naked, trapped in a dead stare.

I hated Angela's mom. She never gave me a chance and rejected everything we had been building. I'd never met Mister Jackson, but I could understand why he left her. But somehow, someway, I'd get her on my side so that Angela would slide the ring back onto her finger.

The water stopped running.

Shawna turned silent as well.

I patted her, whispering, "Baby feel better?"

I was on the verge of yanking the ring from the toilet when Shawna trembled. Her body stiffened, lurched. My back caught the pour of spit-up from her mouth, and I whipped around. From the mirror on the medicine cabinet, I watched banana-apple sauce sliding into my tank top. I peeled off my shirt and dropped it with my shorts. Another long night was ahead.

She cried as I carried her to the room. Cried as I laid her down on the futon. Cried as I rummaged through her bag. Cried as I pressed the heart-shaped thermometer to her forehead.

The temperature reading on the sticker began in the yellow section: a subnormal temp. The ER doctor from early Thursday morning directed a return for antibiotics if the numbers went into the red bars.

Shawna was sweating, but I wasn't sure if it came from the fever, or the weather. Maybe we shoulda left for the hospital already? The numbers climbed into the faint green section: a low-average temperature.

Lately, my car had been running hot, so I wasn't sure if we would make it. After the arrest last year, my plastic was maxed out. My bank account couldn't cover a visit copay, meds, and an Uber.

I brushed the hair off her temple. Shawna felt fine to me, but maybe that had been wishful thinking. The sticker went dark green, and I crossed my arms because the next section would be red.

She continued to cry.

Before our ER visit earlier this week, baby girl had been extra irritable. She woke up vomiting, and everything I had that was absorbent—bath towels, drool rags, paper rolls—was already drenched. As I drove her to the hospital, it was past midnight and all I had to wipe her mouth was toilet paper. Once she was admitted, I texted Angela with a complete update. Baby girl had an earache, but the IV hydrated her. I assured Ang everything was fine since I knew she had to work before school.

No sooner did Miss Jackson arrive. Frazzled. Pink peacoat over PJs.

"What's her temperature? Will she be hospitalized? Why didn't you call me?"

Miss J never greets me. It's always question after question. Had she listened to her daughter, she woulda known all the answers. But, no. At two in the morning, her dramatic ass pestered the doctor and the nurses. My incisor teeth clamped my gums when she reported back everything I already knew.

Perhaps, her green contacts erased me from her vision. Maybe from her perspective, she imagined Shawna suspended in midair, floating next to the baby scale, being held up by an invisible ghost, the same ghost who'd been changing her granddaughter's diapers since birth.

My chest tightened on sight of her fake eyebrows and bedazzled fingernails. She stroked Shawna's hair and stood too close for comfort. Her palm transferred raw energy through my daughter's body. When the rough fabric of her peacoat grazed me, I could barely resist throat popping Miss Jackson. Instead, I stared at the bright tile and reminded myself that Miss Jackson was her grandma and that I had to kill her with kindness.

That night sucked, and Friday night was about to suck harder. The numbers climbed on the heart thermometer. I loved my daughter, but her fussiness outmatched my endurance. While she cried, I felt dumb. Tired. Defeated.

I looked to my back exit and recalled when Chewbacca went through the doggy door. I was tempted to escape for five minutes, regroup. But an arrest for indecent exposure would not help anything. The thought of interacting with Miss Jackson in another reception room pinched my Adam's apple.

At that point, after ten months of not smoking weed, I mentally searched the studio for a hidden stash. My mind zapped toward each nook and cranny for relief.

Kitchen cabinet!

I stepped away from Shawna and reached into the cupboard. A case the height of a bong was tucked into the corner behind her food jars. It was a bottle of Courvoisier VSOP my uncle had given me as a birthday gift.

"That'll grow your gorilla nuts," he had said, "and help you get the monkey again. Just wear a condom this time."

While baby cried, I stripped off the gold foil. The nubby cork slipped out from the neck, and I poured myself a shot. A heavy shot. It was the heavy shot of a certified man: mortgage payment, garage tools, broken edgers.

Fumes teared my eyes. That first drink woulda run twenty dollars at a club. To double my money, I swigged another.

I returned to my daughter and braced myself for the final reading. I checked the thermometer and wasn't sure if I was reading it correctly. I rubbed the sticker across her forehead to be sure.

Her temperature had stopped in the dark green zone: a regular temperature.

I picked up Shawna and smooched her cheek. I spun naked, more stoked than the first time I landed a kickflip. Then I worked overtime to bring her cry down. Although we were not out of the woods, I let out a sigh, followed by a long, deep breath through the nose.

"Daddy stinks," I told her. I hadn't showered for two days. "Bath time, bath time."

But before we went to the tub, this good daddy was desperate to calm his daughter. I carried her into the kitchen and sat her on the counter. My pinky dabbed the Courvoisier and rubbed her gums. Warm, ridgy.

Shawna jerked, not liking the taste. Her lips smacked.

I repeated the motion because I needed rest. Sometimes good parents do bad things for sleep.

But then I imagined a meme with my mugshot and a news link. If the hospital requested bloodwork, trying to explain the alcohol in her system would be tough. Yet parenting instincts said another numbing drop wouldn't hurt her. And for good measure, I took another shot.

Buzzing, I removed her diaper in the bathroom. The water ran and I glimpsed my face in the mirror. My regular brown eyes were the same, but I looked different. Even though I had always been husky, dealing with a teething infant made me drop weight. My cheekbones protruded, and my skin looked pale, yellow. That twenty percent Vietnamese in me was representing.

When I had done a genetic test, every major continent was circled except Antarctica and Australia. Basically, my ancestors got down with whatever looked good on the other side of the river, crossing oceans and state lines to visit different area codes. Four generations of Clarksons in this city continued this tradition. Our family is as mixed as a jury duty. At reunions, my darker-toned fam hangs out in the garage, while those needing a tan soak up the driveway sun. But caramels like me? We bounce around and blend in wherever we go.

As I get older, my appearance changes. Faster at certain times than others. If I shave my head and stay indoors all winter, I look like a white boy. Lose too much weight and slam on a tight baseball cap, I look Asian. Bake in the sun for a summer vacation, I'm black. Add a little weight gain and taco trucks greet me in Spanish. And if I get really fat, straight-up Samoan.

People don't believe that my black hair with a heavy bend used to be blond. Red freckles sprinkle my cheeks like a dog's belly, so when strangers ask my background, I tell them straight up, "I'm a Long Beach mutt."

My bathroom floor smelled. The crumbled grout at the base of the tub exposed layers of curled linoleum, releasing decades of trapped mildew that disregarded any amount of bleach dumped into the mop bucket. But a few pumps from Shawna's no-tear bubble bath sweetened the air.

The foam grew. I hand-tested the water and slid into the bubbles behind her chair. Baby's feet stomped, hands swatting. I joined the splashing then massaged her neck. My finger pads stroked her scalp, slathering the shampoo thick as a swimming cap.

I leaned back Shawna's seat toward me, and the suction cups gave way. I poured water along her hairline, and her tense frame relaxed. Shawna's upside-down face resembled a guppy. Her puffy top lip which reminded me of her mom.

Back when Angela lived here, we would bathe

together. Her growing belly rounded above the waterline like an island. She would gather bubbles to costume her face with a soapsuds mustache. With a packed-on beard, a bubbly eyepatch completed her pirate look.

"Shiver me timbers," she would say, hand gliding down my thigh. "I'm searching for me booty. Ahoy, Matey! What's this I discovered? Why its peg-leg I've been missing, *arr.*"

I wiped baby's forehead with the washcloth that cleaned her body as a newborn. Thank God she's past that phase. I've never told anyone this but giving her baths in the sink freaked me out. While supporting her neck, I'd worry the water might blister her delicate skin. I'd imagine the soft spot on her head becoming soggy enough to loosen, dissolve. But now that she's almost a big one-year-old, Shawna can feed herself sliced grapes. The other day, she turned the page on a cloth book.

I washed my pits while she played with her floating toys, babbling to no end. When she giggled—something she hadn't done all week—I couldn't believe my ears.

Baby girl's bath time ended. My wrinkled fingertips lifted her, and a spray of goosebumps lifted across her shoulder blade. Every towel was dirty, so I wrapped Shawna in my bathrobe. Upon the open futon, I strapped on her diaper and Superwoman pajamas. Then I slid into my last pair of clean shorts and gray tank top.

To help it dry quicker, I brushed her hair. While she voweled slobbery syllables, a yawn came through. My breath stopped. It wasn't even nine o'clock yet. We might get some good sleep which was needed. Shawna could not look exhausted in the morning since Miss Jackson would never let me hear the end of it.

My fingers slid down my daughter's face. I talked to her, slower and slower. Her little eyes opened. She knew what I was trying to do, and her whimper resembled the one from early Thursday morning. Before she could whine, I picked her up. I didn't know any nighttime lullabies, so I hummed whatever came to mind.

As a last-ditch effort, Shawna bucked. I patted her with a heavy hand. She released a big sigh, and her face rested against my neck. Tiny, defeated tears wet my stubble. I knew better than to lay her down immediately, so I rocked in the middle of the shoebox.

Gnarly day, I thought, and wiped the tears off her face.

Her breathing steadied, and I stopped moving for a minute. I feeling in my chest told me I was doing my job in life.

I returned to the kitchen with her to drink a little more. We'd be knocked out together soon. I replaced the bottle inside the cupboard.

My hands secured her on the futon.

"Goodnight, my little princess."

With my bundle of love taking deep breaths, I could let go of it all: the late nights, the crying, the ER visit. There was so much to do the following day as well. I had to get Shawna to her mom. Then do all the laundry. Shopping. Cleaning. Deliveries. And celebrate my birthday.

I barely remembered to set the alarm on my tablet, but as soon as my head hit the pillow, an image of the teething ring in the toilet floated to mind. I would handle that in the morning because the liquor had me mellow. The blasting TV next door drifted away, and I fell asleep with the lights on.

I had a dream that I was competing again. My name was being called over the PA system. But I needed a helmet from a specific vendor.

"Here," I said, shoving my card forward.

"No EBT," he said from under his tarp.

I switched to my Visa. I needed that helmet to enter the event and make money.

"Where's your mask?" he said.

"Mask?" I protested. "But we're outside."

"Mask up," he said. "Or knuckle up."

The argument escalated.

No sooner was I awoken inside my apartment by the neighbors. He was screaming at his wife. She yelled back, but I couldn't make out their words.

The floor trembled. A chase, a thud. Broken glass.

Shawna's cheek twitched. Her hands squeezed. If those fingers stretched wide, our sleep would be ruined. Half-drunk and half-awake, I jumped out of bed. I would be goddamned if that heroin dealer woke her up—*werp*—*woke her up*—*werp*—*woke her up*—*werp*—*woke her up*—and out the door I went.

CUFFED WINGS

Courvoisier throbbed my temples.

Courvoisier balled my hands.

Courvoisier rapped his door.

Ever since I moved into this complex, Dorian has never been my cup of G.

Angela and I had picked this neighborhood to launch our skate shop. We had searched retail space citywide and selected the Wrigley neighborhood. Not only did that area match our budget, but the average resident income was higher than expected. After scouting that district for months, however, we noticed businesses shuttering. The foot traffic would not be enough. On the flip side, leases in prime spots, such as, Bixby Knolls, Belmont Shore, and Naples, would have to wait until we were able to branch locations.

The district which landed in our sweet spot was between Downtown and Retro Row—the 4th Street Corridor. Before Ang was born, vacant lots had been dark there.

But indie restaurants trickled in. Lebanese, Ethiopian, Guatemalan. They attracted a different crowd than the McDonald's down the street (the same Mickey D's where back in the day my dad's friend was shot). Slowly but surely, the 4th Street Corridor was becoming less ghetto, so our goal was to snag a deal in the city's best kept secret before prices jumped through the roof.

To study layouts, we'd spit through accordion gates, wiping circles on windows to peer inside. We'd discuss which counters to place sticker racks. Some places looked like haunted mansions, but Angela brought a clear vision to our future store.

She was good with how to make things look right and designed a logo to tag over the main wall. Yet if she exhausted all possibilities for a site, she would tap out on that location, never to visit that option again. I was more the nuts-and-bolts side. Cost analysis and searching for online deals at stores with blowout sales.

A month after baby was born, we moved into this apartment. We had to be sneaky since Miss Jackson forbade Angela from leaving her westside home. But her mom took a weekend cruise to Mexico with Angela's sister and her five-year old daughter, who also lived in the house with her. So while they loaded buffet trays with skrimps and lobster tails, I packed Angela's shit into a truck and hit the 710 toward the other side of town.

From the passenger side of the U-Haul, Angela said, "This is the flow."

That's her saying. Her personal version of "It is what it is." Moments big and small got slapped with that phrase, even when Jack in the Box ran out of ranch for her favorite hash browns.

In the case of Miss J, Ang meant that her mom could be mad all she pleased, but she would have to get over it since we were becoming our own family unit. Angela and I planned to marry on our daughter's first birthday, so moving in after more than two years together was part of our life's flow. In those early months of 2020, every little instance, such as buying the kitchen trashcan, gave us confidence that nothing in the world could stop us.

We figured that Dorian was a fellow new tenant. Not that he was the type who sprinted to his car after the first hiss of the street sweeper. But, as we hammered pictures to the wall, it seemed like he was doing the same. That is, until I realized, the knocks on his side happened around the clock.

"Maybe his family is big like mine," Ang said.

Sure. One big, happy fambam. With tiny pupils and bumpy veins. A SpongeBob bedsheet draped his alley window, but he wasn't slanging Krabby Patties.

As I stood before his door on Friday night, the brown liquor in my system gave a damn less what he sold. Shawna would not be woken up after the week we'd had.

The argument behind his door intensified.

The TV crashed.

"Daddy, daddy," his daughter cried. "Please don't!"

I hit the door again.

"Yo!" he said.

"Al," I answered.

"Who?"

"Your neighbor."

"What then?"

"A minute. Real quick."

Whimpers were followed by whispers. Since I wasn't delivering a *Watchtower*, my palm banged against the cheap wood. The locks rattled.

"Why you hitting my shit all hard?"

"Seriously," I said. "Open this fucking thing."

"Mind your business, dawg!"

Smoke emerged from the crack in the door. Behind the drooping chain, his chipped tooth resembled a can opener.

Another tool of his came to mind: the .45 stowed in his linen closet. It's hidden behind a pack of outgrown diapers. I know this because when they mainline, I heard him screaming about it over their TV. That's also how I learned their password and was able to siphon their internet with the code (FBI VAN/ pass!word1).

Through the thin space, he yelled, "I'm from

Chicago! We don't play that."

"My bad," I said. "I came at you wrong."

"Damn right."

"I get you, but see, my daughter has—"

The chain went taut. His beady eyes tightroped the link.

"Hey, bitch," Dorian yelled. "You better clean this shit up."

The door slammed in my face. My ears went hot, and my tongue worked the bump on my lip. A callus from blunts past.

Glass crunched, and Dorian angled out to block the messy view inside. He had been barking orders at his wife, not me.

"Don't ever knock like that again," he said. "Mind your own."

"Yup-yup-yup. But, uhh ... I'm not here for that."

His hands were empty. Same was true for his warmup pockets. To keep things peace-level, I laced my fingers across my wife beater.

"But here's the thing," I said. "My daughter's been teething. Not sleeping great."

I explained our week to him and wondered if Dorian even saw me. Ants had bigger pupils than his.

Across the hallway, the hijab of our neighbor poked out her unit. She's the woman I give food to. She rents alone but dotes on Shawna with grandma love and offers me homemade pastries dusted with powdered sugar. When we met, I struggled to pronounce her real name.

"Call me Awwlehson," she said, her English limited. "Okay, okay? Awwlehson."

"Allison," I repeated, putting my hand out to shake.

She had left me hanging, but with a coy smile and a bow of her head, her blue-rimmed eyes conveyed no offense.

The first time she held my daughter, I extended Shawna between us, reducing the chance for touch. Allison sing-songed in her native tongue, vowels round as Spanish but with added coo. I could tell she was a nice woman and all, but between her gold tooth, dark mole, and scratched glasses, I knew Shawna would reach back for me.

Moments later, though, they chatted with the ease of lifetime friends.

Allison paused between syllables: "Ham ... du ... li ... lah."

My baby matched her tone, and when they played peek-a-boo, Shawna tugged at the cloth circling Allison's wrinkled face. Throughout their reunion, I stood to the side like a stranger, hesitant to disrupt their conversation even though it was naptime.

Dorian tightened his eyebrows at Allison. His aggressive nod shoved her back inside.

"What's wrong with y'all?" he shouted. "Got young buck here acting all loud! Then I catch that old, raghead-camel bitch staring at me. And turn down your whack-ass music, woman!"

Jesus turned water into wine, but Dorian's disrespect of Allison converted the cognac in my bloodstream into jet fuel.

"Look, man," I said. "I've been meaning to talk to you."

"About what?"

Before I could answer, he smacked his door.

On the other side, his wife grunted.

"My ear," she said. "Asshole!"

"Shut up," he said. "Dumbass."

Her steps scraped away.

"See, that's what I'm talking about," I said. "Every night you two get into it. What's going on in there? Something ain't right."

His eyebrows aimed my way.

"What?" he said.

My heart revved, hands struggling to remain grounded. They shook with my message.

"Dude, I understand. They like to give us stress. You saw me next to Pizza Hut cussing out my ex, but I didn't hit her. Man to man, you crossed the line putting hands on yours."

Whenever the Summer Olympics are held again, skateboarders will win medals for the first time. But if blinking became the next sanctioned sport, Dorian would peg the record since he was used to drug fiends backtracking.

"Slow your roll, homie," he screamed. "That's all I know!"

The nuts in my luggage compartment were pickled in liquor, extra swollen. I wasn't thinking clearly. Dorian was older than me, but I continued to lecture him like a little boy.

"I'm saying, nobody taught you not to hit your damn lady? We both rock these wife beaters, but that don't give us the right."

That fool got in my face. Puffed up chest, flexed nostrils.

"Take that bass out your voice, scooter."

His breath was humid as a stormfront.

I sized him up. He had a gut, but I was taller by four inches. I was out of his league—from a different weight class. Not a buck-ten, like his jean-shorts-wearing wife.

Tighter than an airplane door, my right palm sealed my left fist.

"I was being respectful with mine, but now you're making a choice," I said. "I'm only warning you once."

"Warning-me-once what?"

Dorian's arms waved around like an air traffic controller. If he swung first, I'd pull back on the throttle. While he popped off disrespect, Courvoisier took over the wheel, repositioning my feet, because the only thing spinning through my head was, Nigga please.

Neighbors checked on the commotion. With people approaching, my head squeezed. The pressure was enough to vomit from, but there was no turning back. I nibbled on my callous, spitting out a granule.

"You're soft as baby shit," I said.

"All day, motherfucker!" he screamed. "Let's go!"

"I ain't no chick. You can't beat my ass."

His neck vein bulged.

"Your bitch left your ass. With your baby. I should make them both suck this dick!"

My brain went on airplane mode. The runway cleared for takeoff, and my knuckles made a direct flight to his cheekbone. The connection was on-time and the right cross landed with no delay.

Dorian's fist clinched. I swayed back, turning my head to save my eye socket, but he stung my ear. I rammed into his abdomen and he bounced off his door, lungs expelling. Just as my elbow pulled back, he socked my side with a hot one. An inch higher woulda cracked my ribs. An inch lower woulda purpled my pelvis.

We gripped shoulders, twisting into the wall. I leaned down, in danger, but he exposed his front. With a clear angle, I kamikazed his crown, staggering him. Dorian tried to cut away, but I swatted him from behind. He lost his footing and fell to the ground.

His wife yelled with their daughter on her hip. Neighbors screamed to break it up.

Dorian's knee came to his chest. When he reached toward his calf, I thought his ankle sprained. But a short zipper dropped above his shoe.

I spotted the knife: gray handle, black blade. My foot slammed his throat, and I grabbed his wrist, wrangling the weapon from his grip.

Bluop-bluop-bluop. Sirens rang. LBPD rushed the hallway.

Trust me when I tell you that that moment looked all bad for me. I was straddled over Dorian, gripping a knife, while he held his jugular, gasping.

The closest cop drew his gun.

I made eye contact, dropping the blade on command.

"His," I announced with raised arms.

"Yours!" Dorian's wife shrieked.

My focus stayed on the cop. I stepped away with turtle steps. I lied down on the tile.

His partner holstered and the cuffs tightened around my wrists.

"You picking up?" he demanded.

Breathing hurt my side.

"I live here."

He questioned about needles, patting me for weapons. He turned me over and sat me against the wall. I could see him viewing the poke mark in the crook of each arm.

"I donate plasma," I said. "Covid antibodies. Fully recovered."

Most neighbors retreated with whispers. Others, including a few resident kids, pointed their phones to record the interaction.

Down the hallway, Dorian stood handcuffed. His top was bloodstained. They tended to his cuts.

"Dude," I complained, looking up to the cop. "He was beating on his chick, so I ran over."

"You did this to us!" his wife hollered. Her cheek was bleeding from his ring. "You hurt him!"

"What're you talking about?"

"Ma'am," the officer said. "Ma'am, I'm talking to you. Let us handle this."

"You should be thanking me!" I screamed.

"Enough," he said.

They were escorted outside. The daughter tucked her face into her mom's neck.

My apartment door was closed. I listened for Shawna's cry.

"Please," I said. "My baby is by herself."

His shoulder chirped. He pressed the talk button and walked off.

My head dropped. I noticed blood specks in the ribs of my gray tank top. In less than a year, I was going from a clean record to a second arrest. Whenever Miss Jackson caught wind of the situation, Angela would never get back with me, let alone move back in.

The square tiles on the floor were supermarket big. Scratched. The divots were patched with filler. No telling the last time they were polished to a shine. Along the floorboard, dead flies were trapped in cobwebs, forgotten by the spiders that moved out. My plan Friday night was not to stare at the floor.

My skin felt slick as clay. My ears homed in on my apartment. I held my breath, listening for my daughter's cry. If she sounded distressed, I would slide my back against the wall and check on her. I had nothing to lose.

My good ear made out soft clapping.

Allison stood there.

"Shu-nah?" she asked, and pointed to my apartment.

I nodded.

Allison meekly smiled past the returning officer.

"Good," he said, sliding on a mask. "Your neighbor's helping out."

"This is crazy," I said. "I didn't do anything."

"If you're transported tonight," he said, "you can make arrangements with family."

Mom was out of the question. She lived in Arizona with her husband. My parents divorced during my sophomore year when I was 16 years old. Dad later began traveling for work, so they decided for my senior year that Chandler would be the stabler environment.

I didn't know anybody when I had arrived that summer. The rinky dink skate park was empty. The heatwaves reached 120 degrees, and I was stuck inside that house with my mom, who was prego with twins. I was ready to burst from her yammering because her hormones sent her mouth into overdrive. She drowned my ears with enough words to flood the Grand Canyon.

To survive my mom's torrential tirades, I stood on the toilet and blew tight straws of herb smoke into the ceiling vent. By summer's end, my fake smile couldn't be maintained, so I slept through the day. When the evening temp dropped to ninety, I hit the park. But my stepdad was irked that I was out late and banned my nightly skate seshes. Mom went quiet on my behalf, and I could do no right by that guy. He snooped through my room and chucked my baggies and papers. After that, I was grounded with my door removed.

Stupid, I thought, and realigned my bed to greet that kook home. His naked stepson would be spread across the comforter, legs splayed, Johnson and Bronsons in plain sight. Other days, I'd gorge on Slim Jims and Fiber One bars to rip the raunchiest farts inside his man cave before Arizona Cardinals games.

Senior year was a tough time for transferring.

Everyone was cliqued up. It sucked. My teachers sucked, my grades sucked, everything in Arizona sucked. The school almost kicked me out for fighting but after I was caught drunk at a house party (where they found out I had sex, although, technically, it barely counted as sex), I was shipped back to the LBC. On Christmas Day, I was skateboarding in 70-degree weather.

I don't keep in contact with anybody from Arizona. To this day, whenever the chance arrives, I talk crap on that state. At sports bars, I hate on their teams across the board. College or pro. I don't care if it's a high school softball team, I will boo as loudly as I can.

My dad lived in an apartment that was closer to my high school than our old house had been. Ten minutes before the bell, I could wake up and finesse it to class on time. Those credits I had lost in Chandler, I regained through independent study.

Life was better with dad. He did the dishes, I dumped the trash. He'd oven a pizza, I'd eat the other half. Some days we talked a lot, other days nothing. Besides doing my best in school, his main rule was simple: play a sport or get a job. I joined a local food service company making deliveries with my bicycle. Sometimes, people didn't answer their doors, and I was allowed to bring their dinners home.

My dad had become known in the local craft

beer scene for his advice. Word of his expertise spread, and he was flown out as a "brewery consultant." What an official term for a businessman whose wardrobe included flip-flops and faded cargo shorts. He looked like a patron while sampling beer flights, but he chatted with owners about projected earnings and mission statements.

"Mmm, this stout is amazing," he might say. "You could tack on a dollar more and absolutely kill it. I'd lower that sour advertisement over the big kettle and place a community table by the front window. I know a guy who makes them for cheap. Mention my name."

That's why my dad was in Oregon Friday night. I couldn't call him anyway. He covered my bail last time, and he said never again. My only option with Shawna was my uncle. He could drop her off with Ang in the morning, but he couldn't cover my bail.

I could hear mom's husband declaring, "No way. Not happening with my money."

An even longer shot was Angela's mom. With her, actually, there wasn't a shot in hell.

The cop stood over me, thumbs tucked into his gun belt. His mask had slid under his nose.

"Huh?" I said, my left ear ringing. "Can you talk to this side?"

He spoke louder. "What happened tonight?"

Carlo, my landlord, was nearby in paint-smeared jeans. I had nothing to hide.

"I put my baby to bed," I said. "So why would I go, 'Yo, I'm dead tired, but you know what, let me trash my neighbor's apartment?' Look at that."

We had a clear vantage into their place. The flatscreen was splintered, lamp shade on tilt. Glass surrounded their half of the mantle. At least my baby was safe on my side.

An officer exited Dorian's apartment. He held bags of brown. The gun was in a Ziploc.

"Scratched off serial," he said in passing.

Down the hall, Dorian turned away. His forehead had bubbled. Bologna in a skillet.

My landlord left.

The cop asked if I had warrants.

"No."

"You sure?"

"Yeah."

"You on parole?"

Allison appeared. Her hands made a pillow next to her face. She slipped back inside my apartment.

"Yeah," I answered. "Tuesday's my next meet up."

"What for?"

"Transport and possession. I was delivering."

"For this guy?

"Naw-naw-naw. Weed. Medicinal."

I had worked for a legit dispensary, but I got pulled over for a janky sideview mirror on my aged car. Thinking it was all good, thinking I had nothing to disguise, I produced the shop's operator license. But CHP said the freeway crossed city lines.

The cop sucked his teeth.

"That must've been before the rule change."

"By two weeks," I said.

"Any priors?"

"Nuh-uh. But a year probation. Hoping it gets expunged. Process has been slow."

"Covid's backed up the courts."

"Pretty much."

His cell phone beeped.

I was about to tell him that my drug test had been clean. Still and all, the courts required random pee tests.

Dorian was given his rights and guided through the propped entry. I couldn't believe I was next. My hands never touched that woman, but there I was, scratching my lower back, about to return to the station.

Air swam through the hallway, pimpling my skin. My knee lifted, rubbing against my arm. My crotch itched, but my only means to scratch myself was to flap my legs like a butterfly. I stared at the carcasses dotting the baseboard and wondered if the charge might be disorderly conduct, disturbing the peace, or something else.

Units arrived to further investigate Dorian's apartment. They sidestepped the bloody footprints and while cops roamed by, I pushed out my legs and stared at my feet. Nothing in the world existed but my naked feet. I hadn't studied them that intently since I was a kid. Curved bottoms, veiny tops. My toenails were approaching werewolf status.

Time passed and I figured the cops would let me grab my shoes. A flashback hit me: removing laces from that same pair last time.

My lower lip curled inside my mouth. My tongue slid along the new formed skin. The instant I punched Dorian, I had bit off the callus. My tongue flitted the sore.

I heard the cop's voice. I thought he had left earlier, but now he strode in my direction with his partner. Both wore black steel-toed boots with the laces tightened. My feet were before me, but my biggest steps backward were ahead.

I was gripped by the arm, instructed to stand.

"C'mon, man," I said. "I didn't do nothing."

"Okay, buddy."

"She could be dead right now."

"Relax," the partner said, unlocking the cuffs. "You're free to go."

"She never mentioned you again," said the officer. His mask had become a chinstrap. "Apparently, he struck her and went off the rails because she messed up his remote."

"For changing his presets," the partner clarified.

"Changing his presets," the cop confirmed. "She

nodded out and was taken in for observation."

My wrists had indents.

"Your neighbor won't be back," the cop added. "Third strike with that stolen piece."

"You serious?" I said, blowing the skin.

"The kid's in custody," he said. "Social workers can sort that out."

"Before you go," the partner said. "Next time a situation like this happens, let us deal with it. This could have ended bad."

"I know," I said, playing dumb. "Lost my head."

Most of my neighbors had returned to their units, including my landlord. The remaining person in the hallway was a teenage girl. I saw her with her phone before she ducked into her apartment.

When I entered mine, Allison was asleep next to the futon. Her back was against the wall. Her knobby hand rested on Shawna's back. I wondered if she'd ever made a fist to strike someone.

I crept closer, trying not to creak the floor, and I cleared my throat, not wanting to startle Allison. She didn't budge. I tried again, but her snore persisted.

If it was anybody else, I woulda tapped them awake. I considered poking her hip with a broom, but she wasn't a damn animal. I was too tired to care about Allah or Mohammad or whoever else might smite me, so my toe nudged her ankle.

Her eyes parted.

"She fine," Allison said. "Sleeps good."

"Good," I said.

"All okay?"

I thumbed toward next door.

"He's in jail," I whispered. "Not me."

Allison patted my daughter, nodding. She adjusted her glasses then flattened her hand on the mattress. She was unable to push herself up. On the following attempt, her hand squeezed the sheet, arm wobbling. Her gummy eyes blinked, confused by her failed efforts.

I offered my arm, and she latched on. Her hands didn't feel like anything special. Just regular old-people hands. Maybe softer. Her legs stabilized and I walked her to the door.

"Thank you," I said. "Ham-doo-lala."

She yawned, covering a smile.

"*Al*-hamdulillah," she corrected.

After she left, I locked the door.

My sore hand touched my daughter's forehead. Her temperature remained normal.

The time on my tablet was nearly midnight. I reset my alarm for later. By noon the following day, I'd be right back where I was—sleeping after dropping Shawna at Angela's. I'd wake up refreshed in the afternoon and do the dishes. Along with everything else, an order came in that needed to be shipped before I went out with my boys.

I turned off the light and curled around my

daughter's small body. I practiced Allison's word and forgot it again, drifting to sleep. I had a weird dream about weed.

But morning arrived quicker than a ten count, and I awoke to the *fresh-da-fresh-da-fresh-da-f-f-f-*freshest sound in the world!

PEARLY TOOTH

Better than chirping birds, it was Shawna spewing a string of goo-goo gagas. Her baby slang bounced off the walls, switching patterns like sentences. The tender gab was a blessing to hear—much nicer than demands by a jailer.

"Good morning," I greeted in baritone.

Shawna giggled, her legs kicking.

She patted my hand as I palmed her belly. I winced from the contact, switching to my right.

"Someone's happy."

She went on a roll. She replied something like, "I *gaw-da-da-da*."

"That's right," I said. "You got your *da-da-da-da*."

She continued babbling to the carpet, ceiling, and kitchen. Whatever the topic, her opinionated tone could fill a podcast.

"No way," I said, playing the role as her cohost. "Who tried to hit you?"

Shawna blubbered her lips.

"Say what? And then the baby cops tried to take you to baby jail? In little baby handcuffs? Oh my goshes!"

She paused at my reaction. Then she spurted a paragraph. Whatever the topic was, she was serious about.

I jumped in. "But Daddy shook his finger and said, 'No, no, no. Not my little girl. You go away.'"

She continued to gossip, dropping exclusive details to her little imaginary baby viewers. Her never-ending story reminded me of my mom who has visited her granddaughter for a grand total of uno. That's one time, for two hours, during a three-day weekend. Reason for fluke visit: friend's wedding at the Queen Mary.

"Come see you brother and sister," Mom texted. "Only a five-hour drive."

Before kindergarten began, she had me watching *Dora the Explorer*. Because of it, yo hablo español a little too muy bien since the district placed me in bilingual education. On the round carpet, I musta been like, "Hola, amigos! Soy Alejandro. Vamos a la fiesta. Fantástico!"

Even though my mom was fluent in Spanish, my parents agreed those classes progressed too slowly, so they switched me back into regular class. Now as an adult, I don't know what language my mom speaks; she never understands when I tell her that my ride would die on the I-10.

Numerous times, I've told her that to survive on the freeway, my car needs a jack, toolbox, and booster cables. I named my old car Pearly, and her head gasket would geyser in that heat.

Even worse than the state of my vehicle, the price of Cali gas is painful. People may honk at me for traveling forty-seven in a fifty-five mile per hour zone, but I'm too occupied stretching my MPG longer than taffy. The law can recycle their speed guns because the engine shakes when I mash the pedal. Pearly's timing belt needs tightening and there's a hole in the muffler. Amongst other minor things, her brakes are loose and the registration is expired.

"You could fly," Mom reminds me. "And the baby would be free."

Sometimes, I wanna be like, "Shawna might cry. I'm not putting her through all that."

But if mom doesn't care to see Shawna grow, that's on her. She has her own flesh and blood she can watch grow there.

The alarm on my tablet rang.

The base was cracked, but I continued to use it since I needed a new phone. I pressed the home button, and the missing screen fragments nearly cut my finger.

When I rolled to hover over Shawna, baby girl bloomed a smile. Her gums flashed a white line. To be certain it cut through, I tickled her feet. Her giggle confirmed the good news. First tooth!

Shawna destroyed her Saturday morning oatmeal. I sliced extra banana for her and I finished off the mushy, brown end. On my plasma payment card, what I called my blood money, I had ten bucks left. During the drive back from Angela's, I'd grab something to eat. While I burped baby girl, Angela reminded me via text, "Don't be late. Early if possible. Please!"

I wiped Shawna's mouth and removed the heart sticker from her forehead. Then I snapped a pic of our daughter to forward to Ang. But on second thought, I'd surprise her in person with the good news. Instead, I sent the photo to my dad, and he emoji'd two thumbs up.

Since my day started late, I hurried. I washed the blood specks from my tank top, which fit loose because of the stress, and I removed the teething ring from the toilet. While brushing my teeth, I thought of Dorian's can opener fang . . . and the fight . . . and the cuffs. My mouth was dry with thirst, but I wasn't hungover. In the mirror, I checked myself. My discolored jawline would be covered by a mask. Meanwhile, the normal shade to my face, a soft brown the color of Courvoisier cut with water, was returning.

I unzipped baby girl's diaper bag, and a wipee packet fell out. It slid off the sheets to the floor where Allison had been sleeping. I would have to thank her again for watching Shawna.

Miss Jackson had packed a new outfit for her to wear: a pink tracksuit with matching shoes. Sure, her bucket hat was soft, but did everything have to be Gucci? Shawna would outgrow the get-up by the new year, but I had learned to pick my battles since it was two against one, favoring Miss Jackson on Angela's side.

Recently, Ang started to become more like her mother who would tote a Coach purse anywhere, including the 99-cent store. Based on Shawna's clothes, they had plans to drive to a rich area—Newport Beach or Rodeo Drive—to take social media pics. Before the parking meter would expire, an envious location would be pinned to their filtered posts.

The way I see it, because Mister Jackson played a few years in the NFL and dumped her with the house and enough funds for a mommy makeover, Miss Jackson forever fronts, hating on men for being left behind by one. She creates reasons to fight me despite my attempts kill her with kindness, a tactic suggested by my dad who lived by that motto as a former food server.

I grabbed my wallet and keys from the mantle. Construction had reconvened. White trucks were parked in the alley.

Across the hall, Dorian's door had yellow tape. The wall was dented, so the building owner would have to spackle it. I hoped Carlo wouldn't charge me for the repairs. With Shawna and bag in tow, I hurried to my car in hopes of dodging him.

Next to be fed was Pearly. If she is parked in one space for too long, she catches attitude, spilling oil on the cement. The rains swirl purple rainbows in the slick grease. If she's parked over grass, the dead blades may as well say: "Al's Lacville '79 Was Here."

Pearly hates to be woken up. Her dented hood yawned with a shriek of mismatched engine parts. All her hoses are either too long or too short, none correct since I cop whatever's cheapest. I recently installed a radiator with the alternator rebuilt, and those clean metals stand out amongst the corroded pieces. Some are mended with duct tape which I store in the glovebox. Others, I keep together with materials not found in your average engine: welded pennies, a strip of tennis ball.

Mechanics take two stances with Pearly. Either they stare in disbelief and say, "We can't handle that. Too much of a job." Or, they tinker around, acknowledging my method to the madness. When I'm holding Shawna, those mechanics hook me up with little extras.

To keep her running, I will never admit how many times I've paid over her Kelley Blue Book. Salesmen worry if she's fit for the road and won't allow a trade-in. Since I'm broke and can't buy anything else, she's all I got to deliver food and check in at the blood center.

I fed a quart of oil to my second baby. Pearly gulped down the plastic bottle like morning coffee. Her hood slammed shut, dusting up orange soot from the state fires. My left hand felt a little pain when I secured Shawna into her seat.

Pearly was not to be rushed. She cranked up all good, and I pushed the pedal to jumpstart her heart. Twisting the wheel stretched her old limbs, and a pump of the breaks fortified her tendons. I throttled the gas to clear her throat. Once properly warmed up, she permitted me to pull away from the curb.

To avoid my tags getting questioned, I pushed Pearly through small streets. Her hood stretched as long as a football field, hogging the lane. The other cars gave us ample space. A Prius drifted into our lane, and Pearly's blaring horn rivaled a hockey siren. The driver wearing a turtleneck nearly suffered a heart attack. But at least he had air conditioning.

Since October forgot that summer had ended, I kept my windows rolled down. My left arm, tattooed with Shawna's name on it, hung outside. Before the entire country shut down, I was making good money and had a tribal sleeve outlined. My tattoo artist then went overseas to continue making money but promised to return stateside when things fully opened back up.

In the rearview, I caught Shawna in awe of her hand. One finger curled toward her thumb. The pads met, sliding against each other. They parted and her next finger glided across her thumbpad. I was proud of those tiny movements, the complete concentration required. My friends don't get that stuff, so I store those memories.

Shawna began another conversation which led to singing. Pearly hummed along and beatboxed with her usual bumps and crunks, pings and ticks. I was their sole audience member sitting front row in the driver's seat. Shawna's private concert ended, and I woulda switched to my music, but the tablet was in her bag. Then, I did something I never do. I turned on the radio.

I twisted knobs and clicked buttons. The orange needle landed on a station that cut to sponsors. Typical phrases escaped the blown-out speakers:

—For a limited time!

—We have the best selection in town!

—Twenty-to-forty percent off!

Angela's house was a few miles away, and I was forced to turn onto Long Beach Boulevard. A shredding sound tore from my stomach. The compressed lining digested itself. Both my babies were fed, but I had left the house without eating.

When I'm hungry, my mind skips . . . *my mind skips . . . my mind skips . . . my . . . mind . . . skips*, but an ad caught my ear.

MEAT BREE

Meat Shake was a new fast-food joint. While other radio announcers boomed with testosterone, only to then chipmunk through disclaimers, this commercial kicked a funky bass line. Over the plunky riff, a slinky chime cruised the beat. The jingle lulled me in.

"I want to a have a meat shake," a duet sang. "I want to know the secret."

A *yeehaw* commanded the airwaves.

"Howdy, partner! Direct from Houston, Meat Shake's nationwide expansion has served three million red-blooded Americans like you. And soon to take over the world! From the head honcho to the little buckaroos, our combos fit any wallet. So, grab the family and make a visit real quick!"

"I got to get a meat shake," the duet faded out. "I got to know the secret."

I had saved time that morning by not showering, and according to the announcer, their newest location was a block away. A burger would hit the spot with a refreshing shake.

I hit a red at Willow Street and looked around the intersection: to my right, Veggie Hut; to my left, McDonald's; catty-corner, Alberto's; across the street, Meat Shake.

In the past, that building had been a Burger King. But no line ever stretched into the street for a mix-and-match Whopper deal. A smiling cow had been installed on the roof. Her automated tail swung. Cheerful children were attached to enjoy the ride. Across the cow's flank, red neon blinked: "Shhh . . . The Secret's Here."

"You know, hon," I told Shawna. "Daddy could definitely use something to eat. We're early for mommy's anyway."

Wide-eyed, Shawna stared at the children playing inside the giant farm pen. They rocked on plastic calves. Chased over spotted bridges. Slid down a pink tongue. Older kids blasted cannons fashioned as drinking straws to refill the ball pit. The littlest ones rode a choo-choo train dubbed the Moo-Moo Rail with their parents.

Next year, Angela and I could throw Shawna's birthday there. I already found a rec hall for her first party happening in a couple of weeks. I needed to verify the best timeslot with Ang, something which I planned to finalize during the switch off.

We followed the chain of cars into the lot.

Their sign offered three ways to order. First

option: the Meat Shake app; a GPS pinpointed the driver's location to whip up the meal upon arrival. Second option: a height-adjustable kiosk; a standing disinfectant pump provided germ protection. Third option: voice recognition; a digital farmer on the menu board confirmed the customer's selection.

For those reasons, I was caught off guard by the employee punching in orders on a brand-new tablet. The durable case could withstand any fall. He swiped cards, printing receipts off the hip.

The line rounded into a lane flanked by shrubs. The bushes were clipped as drinking cups. A car proceeded to a mini-barnyard as the pick-up window. Small doors divided and robot arms pushed out with lime green hands clamping orders. The mechanical fingers gradually released the bag then pointed the customer beneath the bowlegs of a cow. A chain dangled from its neck and the catchphrase, "Taste the Secret Now," was engraved on the gilded bell.

Considering the number of people there, the wait pushed faster than expected. That was a good thing for Pearly's impatient nature. I was inside my car, so I didn't have to mask up. I forgot mine, anyway.

But out of the blue, my driver's side window whirred to the top, which is one of Pearly's unexpected tricks, especially on hot days. I pressed the down button. The pane bounced, dropping a smidge, objecting. Pearly can sense when a vibe is off, but I was too hungry to notice.

The costumed attendant with a headset was dressed as a scarecrow. Sweat dripped past the crumpled brown hat, and he wiped his forehead with a patch of green bandana sewn to the sleeve. The sun was bright over his shoulder. I'd forgotten my sunglasses on the mantle.

"Welcome to Meat Shake," he greeted.

A stitched smile was printed on his mask. The nose was candy corn.

"Leave here feeling meaty good," he said, rushing through the spiel, "or your next shake is udder-ly free."

Upon noticing Shawna, he whirled a finger. A chicken on skates rolled up. The mascot waved at my daughter and shoved a balloon through her open window. An employee dressed as a pig zoomed past, tossing a coloring book with crayons on the back seat. A turkey added to the pile a tattoo pack.

"May I take your order?" said the attendant.

I rolled my hand, explaining through the napkin of space, "Sorry, my window just broke."

"No problem," he said. "A lot of customers do the same now, considering."

"All I see are shakes," I projected, "but I haven't seen the full menu."

He moved closer.

"I can assist with that," he said. "First, let's get your shake going."

"What flavors you got?"

"We offer savory chicken, juicy steak, or sweet pork."

"Hold on," I said, "I can't hear you." My ear aimed toward the window. "Say that again."

He repeated the information, adding, "We also have our special of the month: turkey jerky. What would you like?"

"No," I said louder. "I think you misheard me. Here, let me try this window again."

Pearly didn't budge. Testy.

"You want a shake," he asked, "right?"

I nodded. "But did you mention chicken?"

"Or steak, or pork, or turkey jerky."

I was starving.

"Naw, that's okay. I'll just take a cheeseburger," I said, "and strawberry shake combo. Thank you."

"Someone knows our hidden menu," he said impressed. "Do you want those fries Buckaroo, Lil Lady, or Head Honcho?"

"Uh, Head Honcho."

"Perfect," he said. "Let me repeat your order. That's a chicken fries combo with a cheeseburger-blended strawberry shake. Will that be all for you?"

"Wait. What?"

"Medium-sized chicken fries. One cheeseburger-blended strawberry shake. Your total will be—"

"Hold up," I yelled, my mouth angled toward the doorframe. "You're telling me, the fries are basically chicken fingers, but the shake tastes like . . . huh?"

"I see you're not familiar with our ingredients. Move forward, and I'll explain."

The car ahead was near the pick-up window. While I filled in the gap, the Scarecrow accompanied me at Pearly's side.

"Initially," he said, "we take a measure of the sweetest dairy creams. Then, we combine it with your favorite meat and toss in cheddar cheese and black beans. After that, we spill our special syrup into the blender and when done—voila—the juicy batter spills, frothy and thick, into our trademark cup."

Yuck, I thought. That sounded disgusting.

"The texture is silky smooth," he continued. "It's kind of like the food a pregnant woman gives her fetus, teeth not required, to build it up and make it stronger. There's not a warmer, tastier option on the market to grab your daily beef."

In the rearview, Shawna reached for the balloon string. I imagined dark gravy dripping down her pink jumpsuit.

"I thought they came separate," I said. "You know, like Steak-N-Shake?"

"I see you're not excited," he said. "The commercial does more justice for our product."

I almost blurted, "Who would drink this?"

But the line of cars down the street answered my question.

In my head, when I had heard him say "meaty good," I thought he meant "thick," like ice cream chunks in a malt, or peanut butter in a protein shake.

"Don't you have regular shakes?" I asked. "Plain old chocolate, or blueberry. Peach, even?"

"Well, we do have vanilla."

"Now, that sounds delicious. Let me just have that with the fingers."

"But it's vanilla ham. We only serve it during Christmastime."

Pearly did baby bounces over a speed bump, her frame whining for fresh shocks. Her brakes squeaked. The next stop was the pick-up window.

"I'm trying," Scarecrow whispered into the headset. "The customer won't pick anything. Roger that. I'll remind him."

The orange circles on his cheeks dropped.

"Order something," he demanded. "Remember, if you don't enjoy the shake, the next will be udder-ly free."

The turkey, the pig, and the chicken zipped past the bushes. Their wheels screeched at Pearly's hood. They pointed to themselves, hitting the flex stance, vying for my pick. Gold worms of sunlight nibbled my cracked windshield. The temperature was picking up.

Agitated, Pearly stalled.

"Fuck," I muttered.

The attendant clicked off the mouthpiece and pointed to the looming cow exit.

"Read the damn sign: 'Taste the Secret Now.' Not later-now. *Now*-now."

Pearly restarted, but was neither pleased with his tone, nor the zoo patrol blocking her path. Her anger bubbled, grumbling under my feet, preparing to idle. My foot stamped the gas. Two hundred horses rumbled under the hood, and the mascots slid backward.

"What was that for?" asked the turkey.

"What the hell, man?" protested the pig.

"C'mon, bruh," said the chicken. "You're stealing my bonus."

Concerned about Pearly, I barely heard them.

Scarecrow's stitched smile met the window. He growled, "Taste the secret already."

Then, under his breath, I swear he called me a "meat-hating sissy."

Pearly boiled over, shaking uncontrollably.

I revved. The animals scattered, and the attendant backpedaled.

"Not now, Pearly," I said. "Shit-shit-shit."

Boom!

She backfired, demanding a nap. No matter how gently I twisted the ignition, she snored.

Click-click-click-clack.

There would be no rousing her. But with rest, I knew she would turn over. How long that would take was unknown. Accustomed to Pearly's outbursts, Shawna's attention was trained on the balloon.

The barnyard window was closed. No arms zoomed out. The view to the street was clear.

"Move this thing," Scarecrow fumed. "People are waiting."

A motorcycle could maybe edge past Pearly.

"Dude," I yelled, "this ain't a Bug. I can't push it by myself."

"Nope," he said. "Can't help you."

He pointed to the restaurant across the street.

"Maybe you'd be happier with those fruity nutjobs at Veggie Hut. You could listen to world music and choke on hemp granola."

The anger went over my head. Pearly's door creaked when I stepped out. My hands clasped over my chest, and their flight patterns appeared. His candy-corn nose became my target landing zone.

But, Shawna's little voice escaped from the backseat. The previous night flashed through my head . . . handcuffs . . . blood stains . . . *alhamdulillah*.

I crossed my arms and tucked my hands away. I sucked on my lower lip.

"He has a baby!" a female said. "Can't you see he has a baby?"

My head twisted.

A woman with muscular arms straddled a bicycle. She wore a lion-printed crop top and hoisted the beach cruiser over the trimmed hedge. Striations wrestled across her shoulder.

"How dare you?" she shouted, rolling her bike. "Where's the humanity in your words? Your actions?"

The attendant clicked the headset.

"Code Purple," he said, pressing the mouthpiece to his lips. "Repeat: Code Purple. It's that psycho hippy from Veggie Hut."

The woman parked her bike behind Pearly and dangled her helmet on the handlebar. Her bundled dreads emerged.

"Brianna," Scarecrow warned, "we don't want any trouble."

The wild pattern of her yoga pants vanished into combat boots.

"'Fruity nut job' is in violation," she said. "No defamation of each other's business, per our agreement with the city."

"You already petitioned," he said. "You already protested."

Her march clobbered the blacktop.

"Lest I remind you," she said, "I served our country for that right. Whether I like it or not, I served the flag for you Meat Shake murderers to be here. But this man is your customer, a provider to his family. How can you be so heartless?"

The woman checked her volume and bent down to my rear window. Her greeting began with a wiggle of the fingers. But on sight of Shawna, her head titled, hands covering her mouth. She inhaled sharply, like a child does before a long cry.

"Butterfly," she said breathless. "My beautiful butterfly. Oh, so, so beautiful."

She stood with a grunt. Her parted lips said nothing to Scarecrow. She tried again but nothing came out. Frustrated, she punched her hip. Again, harder.

"You will," she managed through clenched teeth, "help him."

"Corporate policy," he stated. "Liability issue."

The vein on her forehead bulged. She hung her sunglasses on the collar of her top. The lion on her shirt sported a tilted gold crown. She advanced to the Meat Shake employee.

He mumbled for her to relax.

She stood beneath his chin, and her welled up eyes tracked his every move. Her jaw shifted, temple muscles fiddling. Chick had zero chill and yanked him down by his earflap.

"Ow," he said. "Let go."

His hat fell, and she proclaimed to the side of his head, "So help me, God, if this is my ultimate deed on this Earth, you will empower him."

"If you hit me, our lawyers will shut down your little, pathetic Veggie Hut."

People came out from their cars.

I slid over to block Shawna's view because crazy chick was about to torch Scarecrow with that smoke. Even I admit, I was holding my breath.

She released the attendant. He grabbed his hat and rubbed his ear. Security arrived. They asked if they should call the cops.

"I don't have time for this," Scarecrow said, reviewing the line. "Just push this guy's car."

She snapped her fingers.

"Nuh-uh," she uttered, pointing him to my bumper.

He slammed on his hat.

"Never mind," he told them. "Pass out lollipops and apologize for the delay."

He squatted into position.

"Next time, Brianna," he said, "you're going to jail."

I opened my door. I released the parking brake and steered. We gained momentum, nearing the exit under the cow, but my flip-flop snapped. The plug had ripped through the hole. I grabbed it and continued to push Pearly onto the street.

I had less than half an hour to get Shawna to her mom. If it was just me, I woulda jogged to Angela's, but that was impossible with a baby and a broken Flojo. I stuffed the rubber plug back in, but it slipped back out. I dumped my sandals into Shawna's bag.

"Here we go," I said, clicking her from the seat. I cradled her above the sidewalk. The cement was warm to my bare feet. "Don't worry, baby. Daddy will get us a car to cool off in."

The fee for an Uber would result in an overcharge to my account. I wouldn't get paid until my next plasma draw, which was Monday. However, it would be worth it to not text Angela.

Shawna reached back toward Pearly. Her little hands opened and closed.

"Pearly's sleeping," I said.

Baby started the hucklebuck. Her line of sight led to the red balloon in the back window. I tied the distraction to her wrist with hopes the heat wouldn't pop it. The balloon string intertwined with the long strap of her bag, and the more I tried to untangle them, the more I became wrapped up.

I needed the internet connection from the McDonald's across the street to request an Uber. I needed to get back home and sleep. I needed to clean up. Needed to shop. And wash clothes. Shave. See my friends.

Panic hit as I tried to set us free. How much time had I wasted stuck in place?

"Allow me," I heard from behind.

It was the chick on the bike. She did her kickstand.

"Lift this side," she said. "Now, move this over here. There you go. Much better."

"Thanks."

"I want to apologize. To you and your daughter."

"No worries," I said. "She doesn't know better."

"But she understands vibrations," she said. "Her tiny world deserves the best elements. I'm Brianna. Call me Bree."

Her face softened. She seemed normal. Kinda pretty, actually. Her soft brown eyes in the late morning sun turned hazel.

"What's her name?" she asked.

"Shawna."

"Aww, hi, Shawna. Look at your pretty balloon."

The dimples at the top of Brianna's cheeks deepened. Her teeth revealed a slight gap.

"You must be hungry," she said. "Allow me to make up for that scene with an eggplant cheese melt, or a vegetable paella—on the house."

"Nice of you," I said, "but I gotta run."

"If my bike had a baby seat, I'd let you borrow it."

Shit, I thought. A baby seat.

I'd have to install Shawna's into the Uber. Some drivers had refused in the past, worried about their interior. I totally forgot a mask, too.

Another plan took over. If I put it into play, we could still make it. But barely.

"Cool-cool-cool," I said. "But I gotta go."

Brianna reached inside her top. She unzipped the pocket in her sports bra.

"Drop in sometime," she said, handing me her business card. "I can't tell you how much I'd love to see her beautiful face again."

She blew Shawna a kiss, and I pocketed the smooth card stock.

Brianna squeezed my bicep.

"Please, come in sometime," she said. "That little butterfly is a gift to my day."

A sheen covered her eyes. Glossy, pained. Brianna slid on her sunglasses and wiped under the lenses. She pedaled across the street to beat the oncoming traffic.

"Okay," I said, shrugging.

Was she a druggy? A spiritual leader? You definitely meet them all in this city, but I had no time to worry about a stranger.

I popped my trunk and rummaged through the mess. Besides the insulated food delivery totes, there was fishing gear from the previous owner. Tackleboxes, leader packs.

I dug deeper for Shawna's baby carrier and strapped the Velcro arms across my chest. The Bjorn had been too big for her in the past. She was firmly pressed to my back.

I crammed more stuff to the side, shoving boxes of bearings and kingpins. I worked toward the corner. On the verge of giving up, grip tape scraped my hand. I found my old board! After ten months of no smoking and no riding, seeing the skids on the wheels and the scrapes on the sides was equal to bumping into an old friend in a crowd.

I closed the trunk and patted Pearly.

My daughter was on tight, but I'd have to be careful while rolling to the westside . . . *r-rolling, r-rolling, r-r-rolling to the westside.*

SPRAY PAINTED ICE CREAM

With Shawna strapped like a jetpack, we glided across the street. My eyes swept the blacktop for possible landmines: pebbles, cracks. I fixated upon the curb's exposed rebar. Before the chipped red paint, my leg muscles twitched, preparing to olly. Stronger instincts prevailed, and we vibrated across the yellow corner bumps. Shawna giggled from the *cucump-cucump-cucump*.

"Feel good?" I asked, rubbing the back of her head. Sweat coated that jutting bone she inherited from me. The Gucci hat went in my back pocket.

"Cool off," I said, lifting her mane.

Her legs dangled in puffy sections. Biscuits popped from a canister.

When those chubby rolls melt away, I'll begin her skate lessons. Whether she rides goofy-footed like me, or regular like her mom, my arm will guide her though an empty parking lot. By second grade, she will mirror my pump up a quarter pipe, doing kick turns down the vertical wall, and advancing to halfpipes. During high school, gym class will strengthen those thighs, and her perfected routine will be replayed on ESPN for the Olympic tryouts. In her qualifying win, Shawna will catch major air above the big bowl, twisting slow-mo through the sky, helmet glittering with unicorn stickers.

I remember when Santa hooked me up with my first board: Teenage Mutant Ninja Turtles. The graphic showed Master Splinter karate chopping a stack of pizzas. Cheese webs with pepperonis launched past the trucks, and I would carry that lumber to the backyard.

My pants had patches from knee riding before I learned how to stand. To increase speed, my left foot would kick down the driveway. But I was too scared to drop the tail, and my hands would bang into the gate. I'd push back toward the garage. Crash again.

Bang, crash, bang, crash.

Mr. Mullens next door complained. He worked graveyard at the refineries, so my parents allowed me to skate on the block. Not around the block. Not across the street. Strictly to the corner and back, corner and back, corner and back.

If I was with friends, circling the block was okay, but when the homies crossed the street, I returned to dominate my corner-and-back route. Everyone called me "Streetlights" because I had to go inside as soon as they clicked on.

Riding wasn't my only fun. There were Saturday morning soccer tournaments and video game sleepovers. But nothing leveled up to my love for skateboarding. If I biffed a landing, referees did not throw up yellow cards. If I nailed it, no parents were there to form a celebration tunnel. It was just me and my board. All day, every day. And nothing else in the world mattered.

They say skaters are the best fallers. But our knack for bleeding is never mentioned, a talent I discovered the hard way. My brain devised a trick so unique that no one in the history of skateboarding had ever conceived: I would run next to my board *and* jump on it. Mind you, this brilliant idea struck me while the clouds sprinkled. Double-mind you, I was in worn out sneakers.

On the very first try, my mouth chomped into mom's bumper. My lip dripped a crime scene through the kitchen and for a solid week, I *thalked* with a heavy lisp. Which *costh* me the seventh-grade spelling bee. The *wordth* I missed was "fiasco."

For some, the story would end right there. But soon after, I was back to riding, refusing to quit, stitched lip over braces. Mom said I would break my neck and kill myself. Yet something about mastering moves felt addicting. Next to my blue inhaler, I had to have it every day.

But the more that time went on, the more I

stayed outside. The foul air within 2407 Temple Avenue tingled my kiddy senses. Mom and Dad would funk up the place with grunts and rolled eyes, bickering and cussing.

Fuck-you-this.

Fuck-you-that.

Dad jetting with a bag.

Mom crying in their room.

On those nights, I'd watch TV alone, nuking mac-n-cheese cups. Too young to comprehend what was happening, I skipped brushing and showering because I knew I could.

The first time I nailed a kickflip on the sidewalk, I geeked out from my achievement. I had spent months flicking the board into a spin, but my back foot would snag the tail. I wanted to show my parents my accomplishment, but the shouts reaching the porch halted my steps. The intense argument blocked me like a forcefield from entering their world, so I banished myself to a new one. I crossed the street without permission and discovered the skate park. My universe unfolded. Game over.

By freshman year, that's where I went to make sense. Rite-Aid was my routine stop for Hot Cheetos and Arizona Tea. Once the last syrupy drop drained those spicy orange chemicals down, I'd get jacked up with every lick inside the bag.

But I was a shorty then. My growth spurts were stuck in the chamber. The Juniors and Seniors at the park didn't notice me, but I checked their every move. Besides catching them clear a wall of stacked boards, I studied their slouch against the fence, elbows drooped over the top, lounging. How they hitched their cargo pants, adjusted their caps, and smashed down burritos, chewing whatever burped up.

Beyond those lessons, I studied hard for the next chapter: how to line a proper blunt. Puff-puff-pass, I became one of them, breath visible even on warm nights. By the time I returned from Arizona, the little dudes eyed me, checking on what I did. They tucked their shoelaces behind the tongue and hawked on the stop sign after me.

One day after submitting a packet for independent study, I ollied a trash barrel. My weak landing was not deserved of the clapping it received. I figured it probably came from some little grom wanting to be on my good side. Instead, a girl stood at the far end of the gate.

My sights locked onto her striped socks, banked to her caramel thighs, and slammed back down to a long cruiser board. I kicked up my deck, pretending to check my wheels, but with bodies swarming the skatepark, her face was obscured. Even if I couldn't catch a clear glimpse, guys were nudging each other.

Some skater girls are rough looking. Pepper spray to the eyeballs. MMA chicks from a beatdown.

But then, there's the cute ones. Usually, they take selfies and leave. This girl with her knotted, tie-dyed shirt was probably just that. Still, I ducked into the bathroom to clean my face and scrub my arms. I hit the hand dryer and strolled back out to nail that landing.

I sped toward the green trashcan, crouching, preparing to spring over. At the final second, I noticed that girl had split.

My concentration derailed, and I imagined the steel rim of the can clipping my riser. I hopped off and chased my board across the yard. While waiting in line, I looked for her, but she had vanished. My board then squeaked along the edge of the grind box.

In a corner of the yard sat a brown leather couch—dried up and frumpy. Someone called it "God's Fart." The name stuck just like the spring poking my left cheek.

I took another puff and my spliff clouded the sky. I envisioned myself levitating from the couch, floating through barbecue smoke above a soccer match. My shadow passed over the street that led to the grassy bluff where people did yoga.

In my imagination, I found that girl. She was leaning against the rail, taking in the ocean view, board waggling beneath her feet.

I landed and stepped toward her.

My "Hi" sounded weak, but the "Hey" I tried

next came out corny.

With each toke, my brain practiced dweeby lines. *Nice weather, eh? Come here often? I like chocolate.*

My fingertips burned.

Weeks later, Dad asked me to tag along to a client's grand opening, so I hit the park early. Shadows on the course had yet to slide under the trees, but a solitary skater was there. He used to hang out on the regular, but after signing his first sponsorship, he rarely practiced during peak hours. Zoned in with his headphones, he trained.

Although he couldn't catch air equal to me, his efficient movements served a purpose: to maximize competition points. That was a good choice since creativity wasn't his strength. That's why I liked to smoke. To get loose with the brain, let the moments happen without thinking, then watch them from someone's phone and be like, "That was me?"

I plopped down on God's Fart, reached under the cushion, and pulled out a shoebox cover. I sniffed the flattened cardboard, the one that everybody rolled blunts on. Its weed scent was intact, not peed on by pranksters. A corner had split, but none of the buds would spill off. As I got older, I became a better roller, twisting leaves tighter than you'd clench your jaws after a hit of Molly.

I licked my second morning blunt. But I didn't

light it because that cruiser-board girl reappeared. I wiped the sweat off my face, fingers curled around my lighter, blocking the sun.

Like Venice rollerbladers to boomboxes, she was freestyling to her wireless earbuds. The girl was a shorty, under five feet, her braid cinched by a Cookie Monster clip. But she was definitely in high school. With no tripod to record content, she grooved as she pleased. A hot girl who could skate: wicked combo. She crossed an arm over her chest before whipping out ice skater 360s. She was spinning and grinning when she ate it. Like, *wham!*

She looked small on the ground. I shot over to offer a hand.

"Dude," she complained, standing on her own.

"My bad," I said blunted.

A scar ran her leg.

"Whoa," I blurted.

She pulled a plug from her ear.

I asked, "Knee replacement?"

"Oh, yeah, that. Seventh grade."

Every skater has an injury story. But Angela's took the cake and the baker who made it. She was landing a backside aerial when a stray board torpedoed hers. She fell to the bottom of the pool, blacking out in her own bile. Her femur bone had splintered through her skin, and her heel was wrenched into her lap. The sight was enough to make some people hang up the trucks for good.

Ang became instantly vegetarian, and every Thanksgiving, she leaves the table when they detach the juicy limbs to carve the turkey.

"I'm lucky to walk," she said. "I'm a lifer on this old-timer board, but I always search for new grinds."

We messaged through socials and eventually skated together. Sometimes, we had no place to go, but Angela had a knack for finding abandoned locations. She heard about a Northside spot that I never knew about. We bought ice cream before entering the neglected complex. Junk littered the deserted buildings. Every window was boarded. Same for the doors.

Against the back wall leaned a bullet-ridden camper shell. The holes in the roof aligned with the pocked brick. Ang found cans of spray paint near the empty laundry room. She licked her rainbow sorbet while shaking each can, balls pinging. The caps were missing, so she switched the tips. A purple dot hit the fiberglass roof.

"'Rich Plum' sounds delicious," Angela said, reading the label. "Let me try something."

At the top of the pick-up cover, she wedged her waffle cone against the wall. The bottle hissed, and she coated her scoop with Krylon. She took pictures of the colored melt dripping into the bullet holes.

For a moment, I was irritated. I bought that dessert for her to enjoy, not do weird things to it.

She bypassed the preset photo filters to manually adjust the contrast. Ang created this ill, over-exposed image that could be a logo for a major company. She always did have that natural eye. No security told us to leave, but we'd seen enough. While we skated through the alley, she sent me the picture which became my wallpaper.

The next time we hung out, we jumped on a bus to the dead mall in Hawthorne. That place had been vacated forever. I lifted Angela up onto my shoulders so that she could see into the parking lot.

"How much do you weigh?" I kidded.

"Almost 120 pounds," she said. "Too much for you to handle?"

"Check now," I said. "Clear?"

She scoped for rent-a-cops and then waved me up. I passed her board, and mine was strapped to my backpack. I shoulda worn jeans like she did, rather than my tan Dickies.

"I don't normally take dates in here," she joked.

She climbed into the crumbled entryway, and I followed her into the darkness. My eyes hadn't yet adjusted when something grazed my ear. My reach for Angela startled her, and her cellphone light zipped across the ceiling. Cords dangled through water damaged tiles, some brown, some missing.

We mazed through the empty food corner. Further on down, the hollow stores resembled handball courts, with every wall overlaid by graffiti.

The floor was rubbly, unrideable. I unstrapped my deck, hugging it against my chest. If a zombie jumped out, his head would be lopped off.

We turned into a corridor leading to the courtyard. Sunlight slanted through a hole in the roof, and the deterioration resembled the aftermath of a bomb. A fallen directory rested on a bench. A chandelier had crushed the playground slide. I pointed at the pigeons on the busted escalator.

"Look," I said. "No handrails."

We dusted off the edge of a dry fountain and sat with our boards. I mentioned my shop idea to her for the first time. During that sit, after the birds flapped out the ceiling, another first happened.

Angela said, "Just us, now."

"Yeah, guess so."

"This is the flow," she said, making kissy eyes.

I returned with blinky eyes since the surroundings had me creeped out. Ang moved closer, so there was no punking out.

Our lips met, and we caught a nice flow. The longer my lids stayed shut, the more everything around us disappeared.

Yet I sensed a heavy stare and flinched.

"What's wrong?" she said.

The first thing my eyes took in was a doll's leg. Disjoined from the body, it laid across the drain, the plastic limb clinging to a shoe. A single, yellow baby shoe. Coated in dust. Strap undone.

Something made noise down the hallway, and my mind sketched an image of a felon dragging a machete. He would dismember us inside his basement with a music box twanging. Our pulled-off fingernails would tinkle in a jelly jar for his collection.

"You shouldn't be here," the deserted mall echoed.

"Go-go-go," I said.

We ditched the security guard and vacated the mall. During the transition from dark to light, I saw Angela's board and screamed into the sun.

"Scary, huh?" she said.

"Yeah," I said. Then I shook my head. "No. I mean . . . I left my board in there."

"Seriously?"

"I know!"

"Du-u-ude," she scolded. "You got to be shitting me."

I laced my fingers on my head, accepting the loss of that deck. I owned others, but I would have to walk back to the bus.

I noticed her board. Long, wide.

"Yours can carry two," I said. "We can ride it to the stop at least."

She squashed that idea but asked, "What if I got it back for you?"

"I'd owe you."

"Owe me what?"

"Big time."

"What's 'big time.'"

"Chipotle."

"That's it?"

"Chipotle and a movie."

"Bet."

"Vegetarian burrito," she said, before disappearing into the darkness. "Extra guac."

It was rush hour on the bus ride home. She sat across the aisle, and I couldn't believe she braved that dingy mall for me.

Behind her resting head, the sky was pink in the twilight. Lavender clouds slipped across the window panels. Her neck was smooth, long muscles joining between the collar bone. With each inhale, the skin at the base darkened, shallow enough to plant a thumb. My eyes bunny hopped to her dusty Vans. The checkered pattern filled in with dirt. Because of those size sevens, I got to keep my board. I knew then I had found my ride-or-die.

Shawna and I were a mile away from Meat Shake when I realized my bare feet were on that same board. The wheels spun on the pavement. Good times with Angela rushed to my brain even faster.

But before my heart could reopen, truth smacked me solid: I'm not what Ang wants.

As simple as repeating the words *I do*, her mind became easy to read. While growing up, Ang's mom stripped her crayon box to a singular black stick. Therefore, the best Angela could do was sketch a dull future, never envisioning the bright particulars of her personal quest. When Angela skated the city with me, she was rebelling against Miss Jackson who had tossed her colorful dreams of becoming an interior designer, which included our shop plans, into the trash.

When that nose swab tickled my brain and returned positive for the Rona, Angela's mom reconvened her preach for her daughter to find a man in uniform: a cop, a soldier, a forest ranger. Not someone like me.

I refuse to strap khaki pants across my nipples with a worn-out belt. I'm not wearing churchy shoes to a hundred-hour cubicle job just so that I can collect heart attacks like broken lawnmowers. Rather, these Levi's will slant across these hip bones the way I like, and the holes in these shoes will stroll down any street they please.

Being bored for another four years inside a classroom in order to receive what? A piece of paper that guarantees nothing but debt? It's not happening. Soon enough, I will jumpstart my own business because everything I need to know is on the internet. And the best teacher—personal experience—has my lesson plan lined up. After that, I'll be able to afford commercial pilot training.

Although Angela used to be adventurous, the

lockdown changed her. The first stimulus check calmed her down, but after the George Floyd riots, we know our store would have to wait. Inevitably.

She reminded me that she gave up a year of possible school to have the baby and to open the store. It didn't help that while I was out making deliveries all day, she stayed inside getting scared by the news channels. Before she flowed back to Miss Jackson's, I was already sleeping on the futon by myself. Once her bed and the cradle were out, she treated the shoebox like one of the store lots she saw no future in; she never came back.

Her creative ambitions flatlined, and she enrolled into a legal assistant program. For her now, so long as her future man's shirt comes from the cleaners with a stiff collar, polyester pants hard pressed with pleats, she's wet. Soaked. Drenched. Readjusting girls like that is impossible.

They're made by the factory and trained by the factory. They join sororities endorsed by the factory and select husbands from frats so that they can marry inside the factory, cream inside the factory, and nine months later, their legs export another worker into the factory. And the assembly line continues, producing generations of white-picket-fence lives with candles on the mantle matching the drapes.

Even though I know all of this to be true about her, I think we should try again. At least for

Shawna's sake. Because I know how hard it is to live between parents. Sometimes, I wonder how I could meet Angela halfway. Maybe I could work corporate for a skating company since they're located up and down the West Coast. But then again, maybe not.

I shoulda been paying attention to the ground. A pain shocked my foot, the tender underside, and I bailed with quick feet. Shawna's bag slid around my neck. My hands reached behind my head.

"You good, babes?"

Shawna bounced, enjoying.

I checked my blackened heel. An orange dot stained the skin. The guilty party was a palm tree kernel: shell scraped, seed exposed.

I rubbed the pain away and viewed the upcoming bridge. No other route was possible into the deep westside. Before crossing over the flood control and the freeway, I wiped Shawna's lips. Had it been the day before, her drool woulda dragged in the wind.

The sidewalk on the overpass was thin. The railing was short with a section of the barrier missing. The yellow tape acting as replacement spun like jump rope. On a vertical bar, two skateboards were zip tied into a cross.

"RIP LUCA" was tagged on top.

The kid's name bounced through my head. I knew of a Lucas, and I knew of a Luke, who we called Loc, but not Luca. The memorial flowers were old, the candles blackened.

Ahead of us, a homeless man crawled out of the underpass. He proceeded in our direction with a roll of carpet on his shoulder. I envisioned tiny Tech Decks left on the bridge in Shawna's memory, so I hopped onto the street. A truck honked.

"Move," yelled the driver. "To the side."

I drifted to the right.

"My bad," I mouthed.

He roared onto the 710 freeway. The smoky trail burned my eyes. That old truck was probably related to Pearly. Her grandpa, or something.

On the other side of the bridge, we passed an auto shop that had rejected her. The barking dog behind the fence scared Shawna. From the opposite direction, an old woman traveled on a motorized wheelchair. I leaned right to offer more space on the sidewalk. Shawna's bag swayed, hitting the chain link, and the Doberman pounced to nip a corner.

"Dumb fucking dog," I said.

He barked, gums showing.

I swatted the rusted fence and made a stop before an abandoned barbershop. I patted Shawna's back and said, "It's okay, babes."

A tongue of nylon dropped from her bag. Some of her Pampers were ripped, so I tossed the ruined diapers.

Just then, a familiar rumbling seized my ears. On everything I'm about, when I'm ninety-years old, I'll need a neck brace every time I hear a skate crew.

They charged up the street tossing a frisbee. With every pass, they strived to outdo each other. Side flings. Behind the back. Between the legs. One guy tried to catch it with his middle finger, but the pink frisbee fell. They laughed harder than if he had nutted a landing. I didn't get what was so funny. On the other hand, my friends and I were the same way, constantly doing dumb shit on the roam. The mechanic shop-dog chased the crew along the fence.

The guy in a Misfits shirt scooped up the toy. He spun it above his head, pretending to whirl a pizza, until the tallest kid snatched the disc. He folded the cloth frisbee into a full-blown taco, tearing the shell with exaggerated bites.

On closer inspection, the "frisbee" had a brim.

I reached for my back pocket. Empty!

Miss Jackson would kill me if Shawna's outfit was not complete. I couldn't let them pass without saying something. Yet, with a Bjorn and a torn baby bag, acting hard was out of the question.

"Hey, yo!"

The three stopped.

Misfits nodded.

I pointed to Shawna's head.

"We were on that bridge," I said.

The guy in a Spitfire sweatshirt was the shortest. His gravelly voice asked, "What happened?"

The tall dude said nothing. He had at least five inches on me. His tight face checked my board. He stared me up and down, taking in my bruised hand. In his eyes was this strange, concentrated look.

"That's hers," I said. "It musta fallen out."

"Is this real Gucci?" asked Spitfire.

The tall one glanced at my bag.

"Her other grandma bought this stuff," I said. "Trust me, I can't afford that. My car just died, my flip-flops broke, and—"

"We got you," said Misfits.

"No worries," agreed Spitfire.

He extended the cap while the dog yapped. Before I could grab it, tall dude snagged her hat. His face remained serious.

With a wall of traffic at my back, I was trapped. Panic set in. I once got jumped for my Halloween candy, but this was worse since I had my daughter. Maybe a Samaritan coming off the bus would come to my rescue.

Until then, I could throat-pop Misfits and make light work of Spitfire. With the tall one, my best option was to race toward the liquor store. His long strides would catch up, but if I had enough time, I could rummage the bag and throw baby powder in his face. If not, I'd take cover on the ground over Shawna.

I watched his hands. They were a size that could make a grown man feel like less of one. His giant paws spanked Shawna's cap, and he wiped the sides clean. He dished it over with a kind smile.

"Good looking out," I said.

He gestured to his face.

"Oh, man," I explained. "I got into it last night with my neighbor. He was hitting his bitch and—"

His head shook to stop me. His long fingers swirled around his face then motioned toward Shawna.

"She's dirty?" I said. "Let me get something to clean her with."

I remembered the wipee packet had fallen to the carpet during the morning rush.

"My brother don't talk," said Misfits. "He's just saying like, umm, she's pretty."

Unsure how to respond, I stuck my thumb up.

"He already knows what you said," announced Misfits. "He reads lips all day."

"I appreciate you," I said, shoving the hat through the rip in her diaper bag. "I need to get her to her mom's."

They asked how far I had to go.

"Over by the donut shop with the bomb burgers."

They knew I meant Santa Fe and Wardlow.

Tall dude did more hand stuff, and Spitfire replied with similar moves.

Misfits followed the conversation and said, "You sure, dawg?"

His brother clicked his teeth. He looked toward Shawna then back at him.

"You're right. It ain't that far. Alright," Misfits said, turning to me. "My brother wants to know what size shoe you wear."

Under normal circumstances, that question would be all bad, especially if I was riding the bus with nice kicks. But before I knew it, Shawna and I were being caravanned by the crew. Spitfire and Misfits scouted the lane to point out fallen branches. The tall one trailed, ready with those mitts in case of a stumble. He let me borrow his SB Dunks, his balled-up socks bulging in his pockets. We broke off from Willow Street and powered through residential area. His shoes gave me the confidence to take bigger kicks. The insides weren't that wet.

Without cars honking at us, the experience was mellow. The fabric from Shawna's bag flapped in the breeze. I stuffed the cloth back in and listened to Shawna's happy gurgle.

Along the trek, at least ten other grinders linked up. I scrutinized their boards, itemizing their gear. At least seven grand worth of product was floating around.

I asked them, "What's she doing back there?

Smiling?"

"Not really," a kid answered. "She's kinda checking shit out. Chilling. Just whatevers."

"Nice," I said.

"She's made for this."

"Trust me, I know."

"Dizzly damn," another kid said. "If you think about it, when you're a baby, you're a straight up boss. Everyday she's like, 'Hurry up and wipe my butt. Now rub my back and sing. Better yet, sucka, score me some titty juice and make me a baby sammich. I'm tired of that messy apple sauce.'"

They continued to riff. Shawna's name suddenly meant "Goddess of Skating," and by escorting her, their heavy sins would be pardoned when they reached that great "ramp in the sky."

Misfits relayed what his brother signed. He had nicknamed me Holy Balls, a.k.a., Nutter of All Great Things. Thankfully, those hand motions were out of my view.

They had me dying, but I had to focus on the road.

More joined us at the front, including a few girls. Their rips off a weed pin blessed my nostrils. Misfits pointed us out, and they came back to apologize.

"Sorry, Queen. We didn't see you."

"Baby is laced in Gucci."

Their peace offering of a toke after I dropped Shawna off was tempting. I was high anyway, not from the secondhand smoke, but from being on four wheels with a pack of wolves, even if some were pups. Just breathing in that freedom with my daughter made me grin. I wondered what my own friends were up to. They would trip out when I told them about skating with Shawna and this group.

The skating crew carved a left to Silverado Park. Angela and I had been there a few times. She showed me the bench that her sister would watch her from. The neighborhood boys would check her sis out, including the one who later knocked her up.

But there was no time to reminisce. I had less than five minutes left to make it, and Miss Jackson was a stickler for being on time with her granddaughter.

"Close enough," I said. "Gotta keep rolling."

"All good," they said.

I unlaced the Nikes and handed them to tall dude.

I tapped my chest. "You were clutch."

His socks in his pocket reminded me of my nickname.

"When I open my skate shop," I told him, "Holy Balls will hook you up!"

His head shook vigorously. He waved to Shawna and signed something.

Misfits interpreted: "See her on the grind."

"Alright then, for sure."

I thought about Shawna's tooth and couldn't wait to show Angela. I threw up the deuce, and then I kicked-pushed, *kicked-pushed, kicked-pushed, kicked-pushed,* coasting across Santa Fe Ave.

YOU'RE SORRY, MISS JACKSON

I'd know my location if my eyes were shut. The best burgers in town came from the donut shop down the street from Ang's. The vent pumped smoke—beef patties, greasy onions, garlic seasoning—and my stomach ripped louder than cracked knuckles. I had definitely breathed in the munchies.

The storefront window advertised a double, bacon-avocado cheeseburger on discount. I imagined every morsel getting bullied down, and the large fries could get some, too. By the time that combo went missing, stashed inside my belly with a giant Coke, a mass murder of napkins would cover the ketchup-smeared tray.

While fixing Pearly, I would be full because nothing that Bree chick had mentioned would stick to my ribs. But first, it was time for Shawna to be with her mom.

Unlike my neighborhood of apartments, houses lined Miss Jackson's block. Parking was usually fine. But this particular morning, the curbs were crowded, hazards flashing in the street. From her packed driveway, Miss Jackson's Lexus blocked the sidewalk, its butt poking onto the asphalt. Pearly's meltdown suddenly became a good thing because squeezing her wide, chrome hips into those tiny spaces woulda hiked my insurance.

I could not arrive with Shawna on my back. Ideas percolated. The carrier and my board could go between the trash bins, and I could wash my arms and feet with the spigot. My toes could clinch the loose plug of my broken flip-flop while I knocked from the porch.

"Where's your car?" Angela might ask.

"Around the block."

"Hot day," she could follow. "Bring her in."

I'd pass Shawna to her along with the bag.

"I'm out," I would say. "Mad-hungry."

If Miss Jackson answered the door, I'd take a deep breath and remember to kill her with kindness. I wouldn't exhale until the door closed.

I hopped off my board and—*skurt skurt*—halted in the driveway. Music played behind the sagged fence. Heads converged above the slats, followed by laughter. The crowd inside the gate, mostly mask-free, drank from red cups. Hot grease crackled, and the scent of breaded fish lured me from between the cars.

Ain't that a bitch? I thought, because an invite

to the fish fry had never been extended. But if I crashed the party for crispy filets and homemade sides, my plate would be heaped with a fat helping of baby's-momma's-momma drama.

I shoulda walked past the gathering, but I wanted to see what they had going on. My interest was piqued by a picture booth on the fake grass. Angela's older sister, that dumb broad, entered the portable box.

After Miss Jackson had relented to the lawyer's demand letter, Ang's older sister sent her cousins and new boyfriend to the studio to come fight me. But I had spent the night at Dad's to help him with computer stuff. The landlord showed me surveillance the next day. Some of them knocked at the front, while others waited by the back. They had no idea about the doo-doo key, or they woulda ransacked my place. I wished they woulda stuck their heads inside the SpongeBob sheet and become target practice for Dorian. I forwarded the footage to Angela and threatened them with restraining orders. I never saw them again.

The skillet popped grease.

I leaned to the side.

Brown paint flaked off Miss Jackson's garage. A selfie frame was taped on the wood slats. Angela's friends posed with boas and paper mustaches glued to sticks.

Further back in the yard, next to a lemon bush,

a rented canopy shaded older family members. Tied to every white chair were pink balloons. Large, shiny. Shawna's red one became chintzy in comparison, but the banner strung across the alley fence was a slap in my face: "Happy 1st Birthday!"

I was thrown back to that moment when I received a late text on the morning of my daughter's birth: "baby on way . . ."

That was it. Angela hadn't sent the message, either. Her bestie from the hospital did. I left work and rushed to Home Depot for flowers. I was restricted from the delivery ward, so I sat in the waiting area. I legit wanted to bail, but if that baby proved to be mine, and I missed her birth because her mom was being stupid, I would never forgive myself.

Since day one, Miss Jackson had argued that I was unnecessary. She complained I wasn't established. Wasn't making salary. Pointed out that I wasn't in school. Always the damn school thing with her, too.

But I wanted to prove that I would always be around and not a deadbeat like her other daughter's ex. I asked to attend prenatal checkups, but Ang dished out so many "It slipped-my-minds" and "Next-times" that I suspected her of cheating.

Even still, I stayed in that hospital seat, not budging. While her hand was being held throughout her labor, I suffered a series of wondering pains.

Wondering at regular intervals why she broke up with me. Wondering every minute, on the minute, how to pay for daycare, private school, medical bills. Wondering if I should ditch the seat next to the vending machine and disappear forever.

Forever-ever.

I memorized the weather from the corner TV. Hours later, an update arrived on Angela. She had considered a cesarian, but the epidural helped in maintaining her birth plan.

I slid down in the seat and counted ceiling dots.

I removed my cell phone case. The edges were dirty. I wiped it clean and snapped it back on a million times.

I found a plug-in for my charger and scrolled down pages. I didn't hit like, comment, or post anything. Because, really, what would my hashtag have been?

#SheBrokeUpWithMe
#DuringSecondTrimester
#SocialsUnfriended
#EpiclyLatered
#PaternityTestSoon
#IWantToMakeSure
#SheMad

Near midnight, I ate cookies from the machine.

Then the message came: "ten toes, ten fingers"

A half hour later: "look for nurse coming to you"

A mailroom-looking cart rolled out the double doors. Instead of a bin delivering envelopes, a clear bassinet cradled Shawna en route to the nursery.

Everything about her was small. Her tiny legs moved while I wiped the crumbs off my hands. I touched her nose and cheek, under her chin, down her arms. She had the softest skin I had ever felt. But when her fingers latched onto my pinky, my vision blurred, and it was a wrap.

#MyGirl #LifeFocus #ShawnaMarieClarkson

While I relived that memory, Miss Jackson exited the gate. She carried a trash bag in one hand and a plastic flute in the other. Her collagens flatlined.

"Where's my baby?" she demanded.

I twisted, revealing Shawna.

"There's my girl. There she is," said chickenhead Miss Jackson, chipper.

Her green contacts scanned my skateboard like a price gun. She checked the block.

"Don't tell me you rode that thing here."

"My car broke down on—"

"What were you thinking?"

"She's fine."

"No," Miss Jackson said. "Absolutely not."

The trash bag fell. She pointed at me, bangles clanking.

"Where, are, your, shoes?"

Her sparkly stilettos tossed jittery light onto a

bald front yard. Always striving to appear famous, her sashay down the cracked path seemed out of place for westside Long Beach. Her high-heel stride was better suited for a red-carpet strut toward a private jet in Miami.

The leopard spots on her jumpsuit stretched across her gut. If TMZ featured her outfit, her fashion sense woulda received backlash from members of the zoo community for glorifying animal obesity. Which reached the sidewalk first, her curly blonde wig or massive fake rack, I wasn't sure because her cheap perfume beat them both. Yet her appearance reeked of reality TV. If a show called *Ghetto Cougars of the LBC* premiered, Miss Jackson would be lead star.

"Why is her bag ripped? I paid for that."

Miss Jackson reviewed my puffy ear.

"Why are you bruised? Did you fall? Is she hurt?"

Meanwhile, I witnessed her mural-of-a-face up close and personal: fake eyelashes, dyed mouth hairs, dark lipstick, drawn-in mole.

"Hello?" she said, catching me in a zone, and clapped her hands. "What is happening right now? Are you high?"

"High?" I said. "Naw."

"Your eyes are red. And that lip! Uh-huh, you're smoking again."

"Dude, I'm not about that."

My bottom lip curled into my mouth, tongue coaxing the skin. That snafu made me look guilty, and Miss J waved her glass, sipping victoriously. An audience built at the gate, and she went in on me.

"You're filthy," she said. "No wonder you contracted Coronavirus. For all I know, you're probably carrying a new strand. And those needle marks in your arms, you look like a damn druggy."

"You know I donate plasma," I said loud enough for everyone to hear.

Her tattooed eyebrows resembled flapping bats. Gray upstroke, blue downstroke.

"I'm talking," she said. "I *am* talking."

My mouth felt dry as if I hadn't brushed. The dirt swells on my forearms reminded me of the cobwebs at my complex.

"Can you go get Angela?" I said.

"Give me my baby."

Miss Jackson covered her reconstructed nose with a manicured hand. While she went around me, her synthetic curls brushed my shoulder, and I peered inside the plastic flute. The champagne was yellow. Bubbled. Saliva gathered on my tongue, but the spit stayed in my mouth. Despite how crummy Miss Jackson treats me, I always show her the utmost respect.

Miss Jackson cooed, being sweet to Shawna.

"Where's her cap?" she said to me. "I bought

this outfit from South Coast Plaza. This is real Gucci, you know. Expensive!"

Noon just passed, but her lisped speech slithered over syllables.

Gucci became Gooshee.

Expensive, espensif.

"Did you sell it?" she asked.

I could hear her breathing, and I sucked my teeth.

"Excuse me?" she said. "Excuse me?"

"Relax," I said. "It's right here."

I shoved my hand into the bag's torn slit. Before I could pull out the pink hat, the shoulder straps of the Bjorn restrained my chest. I was being tugged backward.

"What're you doing?"

"She's stuck," Miss J said.

"She's not stuck." The carrier squeezed tighter. "Stop it."

Bracelets jangled, and my daughter stiffened. Her happy gurgle shunted, and I wasn't sure if I heard something click. If the buckles came apart, Shawna would tumble backward—cement—brain damage.

"Whoa!" I yelled. "Quit!"

I reached behind, and my fingers slid across Miss Jackson's greasy forehead.

"Chill, dude! Chill."

"You chill-chill," said Miss Jackson. "Why can't

I get her out?"

Her fake nails dug into my back. From the corner of my eye, I spied her thumb and pointer finger pinching the flute. Not a drop of champagne spilled.

The red balloon bounced, and I said, "Let go. You're gonna mess something up."

Miss Jackson's acrylics clacked on release.

I dropped my board to stabilize Shawna. To minimize the possibility of a hard fall, I squatted onto the dirt.

"Give her to me," Miss Jackson said.

I stood with my daughter against my chest. Her back was sweaty, but her diaper felt dry.

"Don't tug on her like that," I said. "Dangerous!"

"Dangerous?" said Miss Jackson. "You could have killed her!"

Her slight thrust of the flute sloshed bubbly onto my ankle. The cold fluid dribbled onto my heel.

"Dude," I said. "Come on!"

"Stop dude'ing me," she said. "Why didn't you call?"

"My cell's messed up. Ang knew about it."

"Did you think to use a payphone, *dude*?"

"Ain't no payphones," I said. "Stop getting loud."

"Don't tell me what to do. This is my house. You're standing on my lawn."

I glanced down at the dirt.

"What lawn?"

The music dropped. More people gathered behind the gate.

Miss Jackson went to grab Shawna, but my board shielded my baby like a wing. I stepped further back onto the dirt, knowing Miss J would not advance in her stilettos.

"I can't stand you!" she screamed, and the high pitch made Shawna cry.

"See," I screamed, covering Shawna's head. "That's why you can't keep a man. You don't listen!"

Miss Jackson flashed confusion.

"Me and your daughter had a special thing going on," I said. "My intentions were good, and you messed it up because you"—my voice cracked—"you are so damn sorry, Miss Jackson!"

She rolled her drunken eyes and stumbled on the busted cement. Like a game of Twister, her free hand touched the ground while the champagne was lifted skyward. Without thinking, I lifted my board and swung the tail, clipping the flute. The plastic hit the ground, and the base bounced from the stem.

To the eyes over the fence, I said, "You see this, right?"

Her friends and family didn't budge. But there were yells for Angela.

"You're drunk," I said down to Miss Jackson. "I'm for real. You coulda caused her trauma!"

"I'll trauma you," she said. "I'm contacting social services. Child endangerment!"

"Here she comes," someone said.

Angela ran through the gate. She looked different. Older, heavier. With makeup and a long dress. Sweeping past the hem were new Vans, the same kind she had promised to wear under her wedding dress.

"Momma, why you crying?" Angela said.

She helped her up, and Miss Jackson widened her eyes, dabbing the corners.

"Burns," she said.

"She's drunk," I said. "She was grabbing at Shawna and—"

"He skateboarded here!"

"Pearly broke down."

Angela focused on my bruise.

"Did she hit you?"

"I should have," said Miss Jackson, patting below the eyeline. Her face dripped more than a watercolor set.

Ang reached for Shawna. "Is she okay?"

"Of course. Here."

She patted our daughter, pecking her with kisses.

"She didn't cry until your mom went agro."

"You're lucky my boyfriend isn't here," said

Miss Jackson, "or he'd whip your ass!"

"How are you in your fifties?" I said. "Talking about, 'I'm gonna get my boyfriend on you.'"

"You hush," said Miss Jackson.

"Enough," said Angela. "Mom, go inside. Freshen up. I'll deal with Al."

Miss Jackson entered the front door. If I had shown up a minute later, I woulda left the premises already.

"Why'd you throw champagne at her?"

"What?"

"That's what my sister said."

"Did she tell you how your mom was pulling on Shawna? All you do is defend that lady."

"I'm not defending," she said. "I want to know what happened."

"Why is this party happening anyway?" I said. "I texted the price for the rec room. You okayed it. We just had to pick a time."

"We decided," she said, "our side is having ours, and yours is having yours."

"Who's 'we'?" I said. "*We* are her parents. *We* never discussed this."

"I decided."

"You didn't decide shit. Your momma decided."

"Stop."

"Be an adult. Make your own decisions."

Angela tugged the balloon string. She was about to say something then shifted our daughter to the other hip.

"We should just do everything separate," she said.

"Why?"

"It's just better that way."

"Is this how it's going down? You do your thing with her, and I do mine? That's old-school lame. Even if we're not together, that don't mean we can't raise her together."

"God, we've been through this before."

"What?"

"We're not together."

"She decided that, too."

"No, I made that choice. I had to. For my future. And Shawna. Because you have no plan."

"The store," I replied.

"Store? You don't own an *Open* sign."

"Right now, when everything is closing, you expect a new business to thrive?"

Miss Jackson's lashes that unglued had fallen between us.

"Look at me," said Angela. "My certificate will be done next year and I'll be working a career job. I couldn't rely on that tweeker-net at your apartment. I'd never finish classes there."

"You know what happened last night with— you know what . . . forget it."

I grabbed my tablet and Flojos from the bag.

"Did you run out?" she asked.

I unlooped the strap from my neck.

"No," I said. "There's some left in the fridge."

"I'll pump more for next time." She slid the bag on her shoulder. "If you'd like, I can drop by your party for a while."

"Retarded," I said. "Two parties for one birthday. See, right there, you're treating her like a football, not the nucleus."

"Please," she said. "No Bill Nye talk today."

To me, Shawna is our nucleus with family members from both sides revolving around her. Conversating at barbecues. Meeting up for Fourth of July. Planning her school years from the same pot of coffee. From how I see it, everybody shares in the responsibility to keep her rooted so that she can evolve into her own beautiful, strong being.

On the other hand, since her father played professionally for five years, Angela viewed Shawna as a football. Positioned on her side of the scrimmage is Team Mommy. Lined up on the opposite side is Team Daddy. Both families wear separate uniforms and strap on helmets, season after season, to butt heads. She thinks this way because her dad gave her mom monthly checks consistent as a salary, but he was never around. Angela can't comprehend the strain of being fumbled house to house, every holiday punted back and forth, landing into adulthood split at the seams.

"Whatever," I told her. "I'm outta here."

I stuffed the Flojos in my back pocket and held my iPad. My arms stretched out to snuggle Shawna a final time. From the first press of her chubby body against me, the grease sizzling in the background disappeared. But when my eyes opened, the yard chatter amplified.

The banner returned me to the waiting room, sitting by my lonesome. All day into the night. Yet nearly 365 days later, there I was, again, standing outside her first birthday party. And when Shawna has kids, I'll be standing outside the same gate.

I kissed her hair and noticed an Airbus passing thousands of miles overhead. Way up there, none of the passengers could feel what I was going through.

"Forget this," I mumbled.

I rushed past Ang and high-stepped the trash bag dropped by Miss Jackson.

"Hey, y'all," I announced. "Listen up!"

The huddle by the gate parted, and I pardoned myself past the baby pool. Parents with their feet in the plastic circle sat taller. Kids shot bubble guns.

"Excuse me," I yelled. "Excuse me, please."

I had the adults' attention.

"For your information, this is my daughter, my little girl. If it wasn't for me, none of you would be here! Now, some of you I met, others I haven't, but I'm her daddy, Al, the one she got 'Clarkson' from."

Someone commented about how I looked.

"Yeah, I admit it, I'm raggedy right now. But my car just stalled, and I'm on a week of no sleep."

The feel of the artificial turf was springy. Onlookers stopped chewing while I carried Shawna past the food table. The relish-speckled potato salad looked moist. The mac and cheese was slightly burned at the corners.

"You never got a chance to hear my side of the story," I projected. "Between Angela and me, guess you could say you can plan a pretty picnic, but you can't predict the weather. However, I guarantee, I will be present on the first day of school until the day she graduates. So memorize this face. In fact, her real party, on her actual birthday, is in two weeks. Everyone is invited. Go to the hall at Heartwell Park. Between the playground and the basketball courts."

My presence would be recorded at her first birthday party—both of them. I reached the garage and positioned my face inside the taped-on selfie frame. Nestling my jaw against Shawna's cheek, my bruise was hidden. I smiled with my lower lip sucked in.

Holding the tablet one-handed was difficult. The device slipped, and my thumb squeezed, taking a photo burst of off-center images. But the final selection would be adjusted, and I couldn't wait to hashtag the shit out of it.

"What are you doing?" said Miss Jackson from her window. "I don't think so. Off my property."

"But this is my baby, Angela's baby, our baby," I said. "Believe that!"

I turned toward Ang. This was her chance to say something. Anything woulda sufficed. She coulda thrown up a hand toward her mom.

"He's right, mom," she shoulda said.

Instead, she was crying when I gave Shawna back.

"I don't care if you apologize a trillion times," Angela said. "I will never forgive you for ruining today."

"I'm getting the hell on," I whispered back. "Away from you and your momma."

The board bounced into my hand.

"Oh, yeah. Her fucking tooth came in. Cut that in half when it falls out."

I kicked off, blowing past the burger joint. In case anyone jumped into their car, I blazed across Santa Fe.

Miss Jackson echoed in my head: "You almost killed her . . . trauma . . . social services."

The thought of social services tightened my throat. Social services meant moms were always right. It meant a chaperone timing visits. Meant apartment inspections. Being forced to buy a crib that Shawna won't use. Being told that natural light is missing. That the security bar lacks a safety release, the temperature is uncomfortable, the boxes cause obstruction, the bathroom smells unsanitary.

My esophagus clamped. An insane pressure pinched my chest. I refused to cry, though, because I woulda flipped out and bashed my board against the bus bench, throwing trashcans into traffic. A 5150, no question.

The pumpkins on the porches matched the sky from the state fires. The hate I wished on Angela's mom blurred my sight, clouding my peripheral. The wheels *chka-chk* clicked the sidewalk squares while I blacked out in anger from thinking the *chka-chka-chka-chka* craziest thoughts.

GRANDMA TIMEOUT

I was so pissed off, I imagined returning that night to kill Miss Jackson. The daydream was thick.

I saw myself tiptoeing into her room, gripping a filet knife from the fishing box in Pearly's trunk. Miss J was wearing a silk eye mask while I stood over. Carpets got stained. Walls got smudged.

I dragged her body to the passenger seat covered with trash bags. Her head slumped forward and smacked the dash. Knowing the little boo-boo on her throat would give her insecurity, I fastened her neck to the headrest. Her Louis Vuitton scarf doubled as a choker, and she resembled a 1950s housewife at a carhop. I imagined Shawna in the backseat fast asleep.

I continued to skateboard through the westside. I couldn't believe I wasn't invited to my daughter's first birthday party. The infant carrier fit loose around my torso as I raced through an alley, shot down a one-way. I knew the cuts where I lived better, but I still managed to lose anybody who mighta given chase from the party. My fury boiled until nothing around me existed. Killing Miss Jackson with kindness had never worked, so I slipped back into the dark fantasy of ending her.

My brain fabricated Pearly speeding down the deserted night freeway. Her engine purred like the day she rolled off the assembly line, V-8 pumping without a hitch. Her speedometer reached ninety-seven while she passed a big rig, seemingly anchored to the asphalt. Her wheels drummed over the lane bumps toward the exit.

The streets were emptier than when Covid first hit, and the weather was perfect for Miss J's bon voyage. Foghorns clanked behind the buildings and dark clouds blanketed the atmosphere, coating the windshield with mist. The wipers screeched from small rocks trapped under the blades. A double rainbow etched across the pane.

Shawna woke up, babbling complaints.

"I'm sorry," I said to the rearview. "Daddy loves you. You're all I have in this world."

Shawna stomped her heels and turned her head.

"Nobody in this world is ever gonna keep you from me, not even your grandma."

The mirrored courthouse ahead dredged up bad memories: unlacing my shoes, my lawyer's gold watch, dad's hallway hug.

"Now, baby," I said. "There's a place called

heaven and a place called hell. Then, there's this yucky place called prison, but to get there, you have to first go to jail."

I considered the possibility of landing in all of them except one. My eyes flitted to the side mirror. No black-and-whites followed. No lights spun in the rearview. But I knew at any moment helicopters could shine down from the sky. Spike strips could be thrown across the ground.

Shawna slid her tongue against the roof of her mouth.

"C'mon," I said. "Don't you wanna help me build a sandcastle? Ours will be three stories. With seashell windows. And an elevator. It'll be just the two of us."

She yawned. Her eyelids were droopy.

"Please, honey. Don't go night-night. C'mon, let's sing your favorite song: 'The wheels on the bus go round and round. Round and round. Round and—'"

No use. Her jaw went slack.

A whiff crinkled my nose. The scent was thicker than a ran-over skunk.

"Oof," I said, "I'll change your diaper at the water."

I turned to the passenger side.

"Or was that you, Miss Jackson?"

I leaned closer, sniffing.

"Oh no, grandma. You made poo-poo ca-ca.

Don't deny it."

I lowered the window and turned onto Peacock Route, passing the skate park. The bluff was overcast, and the pall was thick, as if the moon had taken up vaping. I turned onto Ocean Boulevard and our destination, Veterans Pier, was hidden.

"Been humid lately," I said to Miss J. "Hopefully, it rains. Fish love rain. Riles them up. Dad says bright lures attract them in a downpour."

My fingers tapped the steering wheel.

"When's the last time you went for a dip? The ocean is freezing, but frigid as you are, you love it. Ain't that right, Miss Jackson?"

She'd been bashful since our morning spin began. But for the first time ever, her fake lips couldn't peep a word.

"What's wrong? Cat got your tongue?"

I clamped her chin. The skin was colder than the windshield, and my thumb registered a neck lift scar.

"Yes, Alex," I said, maneuvering her collagens and imitating her bougie tone. "You're absolutely right. I am frigid as the Pacific."

"And should you have been nice to me?"

"Yes, positively."

"Then why did you break us up?"

"I don't know what I was thinking. You're amazing for Angela, and you're the best dad to Shawna. I regret being such a biz-natch to you."

"For once," I said, "we fully agree."

In the Saturday afternoon sun, I continued skating toward Pearly. My board climbed onto the bike path next to the cemented stretch of the LA River. But the torrent of disgust for Miss Jackson dragged me back into my dark thoughts.

I visualized punching Pearly through a red light. The jolt pressed Miss Jackson into the headrest, her skull crinkling the plastic. I eased off the gas, and her head nudged forward. Her jawbone had become rigid.

"If you're tired of talking," I said, clacking her teeth shut, "that's fine. You can nod or shake."

Worried that she hadn't heard me, I pumped the brakes.

"Do you un-der-stand me?"

She nodded, nodded, nodded.

"Good. Now answer me this. Should I have been invited to that party?"

I tapped the brakes twice.

"Were you wrong to grab Shawna?"

Brake pad, brake pad.

"Are you ugly?"

Brake light, brake light, brake light.

"Did you need to stick your nose in our business?"

For that answer, I shook the wheel, and her head followed the motion.

"Did you ever support our plans?"

Swerve, swerve, swerve.

"Do you know your granddaughter's favorite song?"

That question stumped Miss J.

"The windshield should give you a hint" —I jerked the wheel—"'The wipers on the bus go swish-swish-swish. Swish-swish-swish. Swish-swish-swish.'"

Her head lolled onto my shoulder. I closed her lids then shoved her cranium against the passenger window.

"Good heart-to-heart," I said. "Much needed."

The wind fluffed Shawna's hair. Thank God she was too young to speak. Her only witness statement would be, "Nan-a-boo, goo-goo, ga-ga."

My skateboard raced toward Willow Street. I flowed beneath the underpass that smelled of pee. On the other side, I hopped off my board to climb a dirt embankment. The concrete lamppost on the bridge reminded me of the pier, and I envisioned Pearly parked at the end of the landing.

"Grandma had a little scratch," I imagined explaining to Shawna. The drenched fabric of Miss Jackson's neckpiece required explaining. "She spilled ketchup on her jammies, but the saltwater will wash it out."

I dragged Miss J by the wrists, pulling low and away. We passed the bait shop, and the metal sinks brought up good memories with my dad. He would rip the gills down from the tongue, and my small fingers scraped out the remains. I loved watching the purple guts fall through the open pipe, chumming the chop.

An empty flag hook rapped against a metal pole, and Miss Jackson's Porta Potty stench trailed off. I squatted to heave her over, but something nicked my thigh. The filet knife had cut through my pocket. I set the blade on the ground and heard Shawna release a disoriented cry from the car.

I sat Miss J criss-cross applesauce with her back against a cement bench. Beside it, there was a broken pole in the trash bin. I jammed the rod between her legs, angling it against the railing.

I went over to Pearly and brought Shawna out. The winds stunned her. She burrowed her face into my pec.

"I know what you're thinking," I whispered, cupping her ear. "It's kind of late to go fishing, but you know your grandma. She likes to do crazy things, and if she doesn't get her way, she can be a little bi—uhh, she throws a fit."

We returned behind Miss Jackson. The top rung of the pole hung over the water.

"Catch anything?" I said.

Her hunched body resumed with the cold shoulder.

"Not yet?" I said. "Well, Shawna is here. Care to say anything?"

Miss Jackson didn't move. Not a muscle twitched.

Shawna murmured in her direction.

"Grandma's too sleepy to hear you," I said. "But don't worry. Daddy made her a nice bed at the bottom of the ocean. Wait, what's that, grandma? You wanna show us how far you can float? Okie dokie."

I tossed the fishing pole then sat Shawna on the bench. When I turned around, baby girl had beelined to the blade.

"Daddy's play toy," I said, catching her wrist. My tone alarmed her.

"Knife," I explained, and shredded the air above my hand. "Owee, owee."

I flung the weapon into the dark waters and swept my shoe across the wooden planks for broken glass and loose hooks.

I grabbed Miss Jackson beneath the shoulders, pinned her against the railing, and drove my legs up. I've helped friends who were wasted up flights of stairs, but her weight was dense. Her torso cleared the ridge, and Shawna stared at her grandma jackknifed over the banister, arms swaying above the sea.

"It's time for her to go night-night," I said. "Ready now? On the count of three: one, two, fwee. Whee!"

Her legs slid over the ledge smoother than an octopus. A circle of bubbles foamed below.

I swooped up my little nugget and said, "Let's sing together: The grandma in the water goes bloop-bloop-bloop. Bloop-bloop-bloop. Bloop-bloop-bloop. Miss Jackson in the water goes bloop-bloop-bloop. All the way down."

A final wave rolled over her-*eh-eheh-herrr, eh-heh-herrr, eh-eheh-herrr.*

HUEVOS DE TAPATÍO

By the time I calmed down, I was halfway over the Willow bridge. Shrubbery covered that side of the flood control, and whole bikes could be retooled from the parts in the dirt. A homeless encampment lined the shallow stream.

A strip of tarp covered one tent. The ripped-off section advertised amenities for a luxury skyrise: rock climbing, private bowling lanes, rooftop hammocks. The tent was zippered, but a garden fence hemmed in two brown pups.

Outside the perimeter, jumper cables connected a stripped car to a cooking rig. From my junky ride to my naked feet, from my raw hunger to my empty blood card, the possibility of sleeping under a nylon dome became too real, the thought of heating SpaghettiOs on a camping stove for Shawna unbearable.

My sights rose to the downtown skyline that reached higher each year. In the future, I will own a top floor condo with a view of Catalina. When

Miss Jackson starts playing with the intercom downstairs, I'll tell her to suck it while security escorts her off the premises. No matter how much money I make, I'll keep my style comfy and won't need to dress fancy like her. Valets will open the butterfly doors to my car, and I'll step out wearing my usual sweats and slide-on slippers.

Cars passed me and, not wanting to become the next Luca, I snapped to attention. The red light at the bottom of the bridge caused a jam, so I tipped back my board, grinding ply on the downgrade. My sticky foot riding high on the grip tape showed dirty trails of dried champagne.

The opposite light turned yellow, and I slapped down the wheels. Gravity blasted me through the intersection. I passed the green light and bent my knees, controlling the speed wobbles.

On the next block, my eyes caught another green. It wasn't a traffic light. It was a bright green medicinal cross with a leaf in the middle. Even when I worked for a dispensary, state taxes stopped me from buying there. Yet the taste of honey concentrate to seal a sativa blunt was all I could weed about. Oops, I meant, it was all I could Kush about—damn!—I meant, think about.

My three-foot bong was in my apartment closet. The cloudy glass had enough resin to scrape a quick high. Since throwing in the towel on weed, I had the craziest smoke out dreams. There was one where I hotboxed in a helicopter and performed loop de loops over the new bridge to Terminal Island. But then, Miss Jackson's words haunted me: "You smoked this morning . . . Look at that lip."

I had to get her out of my head. All next week, I could deal with the fallout. If I didn't somehow, someway, flush her out of my thoughts, she would ruin the rest of my day. Which was during my weekend. Which included hanging out with my friends later. For *my* birthday. Daddy needed a good time for himself, and that would start with warm food and a long nap.

I struck the blacktop harder. Meat Shake came into view. The lunch hour rush poured out the exit. A cop directed traffic at the intersection.

I skated over to Pearly and patted her hot roof. I tried cranking her up, but the engine click repeated like polyurethane wheels over cement lines. With each attempt, metal scraped, so I lifted the hood. Every once in a while, the fix is simple: ratchet a bolt, tape a wire, vinegar a tube.

If I wasn't exhausted, I mighta pinpointed the problem. But more tinkering led to more thinkering that the job called for my uncle. He hated Pearly. Named her the "Tuna Boat." However, since neither he nor my dad had girls, he has been willing to cuss at AutoZone for a day so that Shawna can ride around safely for the month.

"Anything for Mamas," he says to her. "Ain't

that right, Lil Mamas?"

"Anything" includes oversized outfits and candy bars she can't chew. Uncle refuses cash, card, or transfer, but a plate of crunchy tacos and a six-pack of Negra Modelos has never been denied.

The street sweeping sign said Tuesday morning. I hated to do it, but Pearly would have to camp there for a night. Maybe two. For her protection, everything of crackhead value was transferred to the trunk.

I slammed Pearly shut over Shawna's carrier. The metal bang caught the attention of the Meat Shake crowd. Scarecrow did a doubletake. He wanted nothing to do with me. His straw-bottomed pants shuffled to the next customer.

A hunger pang struck me. I arched my back to soften the growl. The next one mighta ripped me open, so I decided to sneak onto the A Line. The faster I could get home, the better. Hand gripping the tablet, blistered foot on my board, it was go-time! Yet a glance across the boulevard froze me in place.

The bossy owner of Veggie Hutt stood on a stepstool. She pressed stickers to the window: lavender sunglasses, teal beachballs, pink buckets. Her crop top hiked, revealing a large tattoo. Colors and shapes intersected, but the design was hard to make out. Maybe it was stained glass. Or a fruit bowl.

She patted on a rainbow sticker and stretched higher to flatten a palm tree. Beneath her bra, a butterfly spanned her inked midsection. Spiraled antennas sprouted from its head while silver veins coursed the wings. Each section was filled with fresh color, and the tips curved onto her lats. That part woulda stung for sure, but even more for sure was the top dollar she musta paid for that piece.

From the top step, she completed her window mural with a smiling sun sticker. Meanwhile, her spandex pants hugged the contours of her pelvis. Above the waistband, her love handles appeared firm, grippable. But in contrast to her cut arms, her stomach muscles looked faint.

A customer requested information, and before she descended, I scoped out her butt. Puffy, full. During that split second, our previous encounter replayed in my mind: her shirt weighted down by sunglasses, her chest bigger than Ang's, that warm business card she had handed me.

Faster than a drop into a halfpipe, a horny vision unfolded before me: my car sliding down Second Street, dripping with fresh paint. Her pleated skirt grabs my attention and I have to turn down my system. I tell her she looks fine, and she hops right in. Her lotioned thighs glisten on the leather seating while I cruise toward my beachfront home. She glances at me then looks past the cliffs. Her eyes scan the sparkling waves. But as much as she tries to resist, she can't keep her hands off me.

"I need to feel you," she says, and unzips me.

My mind broke away from the vision, realizing I was staring at the slight indent of polyester between her thighs. Creeper. Hoping not to be caught, my eyes jumped to the building's thatched roof from its past life as a tiki lounge.

I was by myself in the apartment for the first time in a week. I thought I had eggs in the fridge, but apart from condiment packets and bottles of pumped breastmilk, it was empty. I hit the popcorn button to nuke an open bag of frozen burritos. I pressed it two more times so my teeth wouldn't break on icicled beans.

My body wanted calories, regardless of the source. The microwave hummed, but I couldn't wait to eat. I considered a jar of Shawna's peas in the cupboard, then wrestled out a crusty bowl among the pile of sippy cups in the sink. I picked off the dry bits, savoring every morsel, but my stomach cussed from the tease. I found a raisin box and tamped an old, hard nugget into my mouth. I drank from the faucet and thought the microwave would never beep.

I slid three burritos into the bowl and tossed the empty bag at the overflowing trashcan. An empty hot sauce bottle poked out the brim. From the fridge, I grabbed my special Tapatío bottle, the one I had packed with serrano chilies.

The red sauce splashed their tortilla backs, drowning their bellies with spice. My hands could not grab their slippery bodies, so I sliced the burritos. The heat from the first strip stung; I spit the steaming piece back into the bowl. I was so hungry that I stirred in the last raisins and imagined them bloating to the size of prunes with each whisk. I jabbed the fork and finally began to eat.

The Tapatío man on the front of the bottle stared back at me, rocking a yellow sombrero and floppy bowtie. He musta been upset that I finessed his recipe. I could swear he twitched his moustache as the shell of a raisin slid down my windpipe. My throat clenched, but it was too late. Saliva picante coated my trachea.

I inhaled to force a cough. Big mistake.

The irritation dropped, snagging down into my throat. I coughed harder than a bong rip, hacking like old timers eating peanuts. Neighbors musta thought the Rona snatched my lungs because I could hear windows shutting.

I returned to the faucet. Gulped. My eyes were tearing when an idea hit. On the Fourth of July, highlights of a hot dog eating competition showed the world champion powering past the record by dipping each bun into a drinking cup. My fork clanked into the dirty dish pile, and I sprinkled water onto the burrito chunks.

My hands moved faster than a robot pulling

goods off a conveyer belt. The wet lumps disappeared with two chews and a swallow. I went into overdrive, stuffing too much inside, and my mouth almost broke down from overexpansion. To pause the assembly line, I turned my head. My tongue cleared a lane for oxygen, yet the trapped air in my chest hurt. My foot stamped until a burp eased the pressure. My head returned forward to shovel more down. If I choked to death, at least I'd be full.

A rust color dripped from my palms. Licking my knuckles coated with the pepper infusion numbed my lips. For the remaining scraps, I lifted the prepping bowl toward my mouth, but the wet glass slid through my hands. The base shattered against the divider, shards scattered. I was too stuffed to flinch.

I shoulda thrown out the biggest parts and swept up the tiny pieces. Then, I coulda mopped the floor and done the dishes. Vacuumed. Done laundry. If I had energy left, I woulda bought another burrito pack and shipped out an order.

Instead, I bridged over the mess and slumped into bed. I stretched my legs on the futon. Squeezed my toes. I was getting comfy until something poked my thigh. I pulled out from my pocket the calling card from the Veggie Hut chick. I viewed the embossed green Buddha and read the catchphrase, "Hi, I'm Brianna. *Ommm.*"

Included were her email and store number. Although Bree had a few years on me, maybe I would hit her up—or, come by to eat someday. But after recalling how she squared up on the chicken, I crumpled the business stock.

Naw, I thought. I'm good.

My studio had begun to bake. It reminded me of being placed on restriction in Arizona. My mom and dickhead offered "permission" to skate in the garage, knowing full well the heat would sap my energy. To pretend the temperature was nothing, I had sat on a beach chair and smacked my trucks on the ground. I nibbled on melting gummy edibles to pass the time. I remember getting real hungry before I fainted. When I recovered before lunch, which included drinking Pedialyte, perspiration overflowed my belly button.

I kicked off the futon sheets and clicked on the fan. The dusty blades blurred. But when I turned toward the wind, too much air hit my face. I switched to medium speed and flipped onto my back. Rubbed my toes together. Then I laid on my side. Folded the pillow. I removed my shirt. The whole time, my mouth prickled from the hot sauce. I thought of nipping the Courvoisier but decided to save the bottle for pregaming later.

Even though the studio was hot, I finally got settled. Having the place to myself was great. No daughter crawling around to find Allen wrenches in the carpet. No neighbors yelling for needles or bickering about spicy chicken sandwiches. I removed my shorts and scratched my crotch. Tugged my pubes. I knew what would help me fall asleep sooner—a little alone time.

Nudie mags never did the trick for me. Slobbering over glossy pages was for dirty, old men. Although I'm no professional, you could shine a light between the gapped knees of those girls and watch the roaches pour out. It had been over three months since Angela moved back home, but I didn't consider myself on a dry spell. In my entire life, I had sex with two girls. With the Arizona chick, it barely even went in. I've questioned if she counted.

I plugged in my tablet. The charging bars flashed—*blip*—the charging bars died.

My cord had been acting ghetto ever since the white tubing became stripped. Through the fuzzy fiberoptic nest, tiny strings were tethered to the USB head. To grab juice from the wall, the cord had to wrap the tablet twice. I bent the wires just so, and my daughter's smile brightened the home screen. I needed to update the wallpaper with her single-toothed grin.

I pictured Shawna at that moment being held by Miss Jackson. A pink cake beneath her fake boobs. One candle lit. Ang's horse-mouthed cousins singing around the table.

I reminded myself to let go of Miss Jackson . . . let go of it all.

My neighbor's internet didn't lag. With free porn ciphered for the win, I watched a video staged inside a mansion. A woman sat against a headboard on a canopy bed curtained with red lace. She phoned her husband, begging him to come home. He promised to fly back when the ink had dried on the deal.

She hung up when a handyman entered the master room. His large glove wiped his chiseled cheekbone, bicep bulging through his cutoff shirt.

He said something about the wine cellar. She replied, *whatever-whatever*, and he *whatever-whatever'd* right back.

If I wanted chitchat, I woulda logged into my dad's Netflix, so I scrubbed forward. They disrespected the manor, sixty-nining on marble flooring. As I tried to turn up the volume on their moaning, my hand nudged the power cord.

The screen went blank.

I rewrapped the tablet and clicked on another video. That one began with the climactic moment. Two sweat lathered men double-teamed a woman on an office desk. Strudeled her face. Then the video reverted to the start of the interview.

The chick sat attentively. She wore clothes: gray pantsuit, white blouse. She was cute. Sleek ponytail. Small, gold earrings.

The first interviewer came across businesslike.

"Your qualifications," he said, "don't quite match."

Her smile dropped.

The second interviewer stood at his side. A tattoo peaked above his collar. He flipped through the resume, agreeing.

They held conference behind the folder, followed by a request for her age.

"Eighteen," she replied with a lilt.

"How are you in front of the camera?"

"Umm, oka-*ay*."

The shredder chewed her resume.

"We have a better position for you."

"Well then, I guess?"

Her voice sounded familiar. Same was true for her answers, which came across as questions. I hit pause and studied her frozen expression—eyebrow arched over pinched lips—and I was curious if we'd met before. Maybe at a house party, or a past job. Or, maybe I didn't know-her know her, but I felt like I'd seen her somewhere.

She wasn't an actress or a singer, but she coulda been social media famous. They're everywhere. I once delivered Pho to a home on the canal. A girl in baggy pants tipped huge. Later, I realized she was a major influencer who had created a viral dance that everyone was doing.

In my tablet, I watched the three of them go at

it. I gave my nuts a squeeze, rubbing them, cupping them, fingers rolling the warm skin.

There was an abrupt transition, and the short man pulled out to grab a handheld camera.

The screen split.

One frame showed her pumps above the desk.

The other frame tightened on her face.

The tall man thrusted while Brianna snuck into my mind . . . her body stretching across her business window . . . her plump-ass cheeks. My thumb massaged the base of my dick. Call up the Guinness Book because a record time was about to be set.

On the verge of my fingers reaching up to play with the tip, the tingling of my balls jumped the border from pleasure to pain. The intensity sharpened, and my nuts felt sunburned. I pulled my cock back and stretched the inflamed skin. I checked both sides for a rash, or maybe even blood, they hurt so much. When I blew on them, each push of air was like water to a grease fire.

My erratic worries continued until I glanced toward the counter. The Tapatío was the culprit. Still panicked, I remembered Angela's bottles were in the fridge, and I considered pouring her milk on my balls to neutralize the sting.

Walking through the kitchen woulda cut my feet, so I searched the carpet for my blue sandals. Instead, I spotted Shawna's wipee packet that had fallen out during the morning rush. I yanked out the towelettes and scrubbed until bubbles formed. The moisture was relieving, the powder scent soothing.

Back when flattening the curve had turned toilet paper into gold, I bought disposable gloves. After a week of my fingers busting through the latex and dusting my clothes with powder, the box went into the drawer. I considered stroking myself with one but knew the rubber would snag without lotion.

The serrano chilies swirled deep in my palm, and wipeeing my hands did not tone down the spice level. I was wary to grab myself, but I had to try again. To match the rhythm of the tall one in the screen, I pumped my shaft between my fists. My bumpy knuckles offered less sensation than kitchen gloves. I couldn't finish myself off, and I had to wait until later.

The video continued to play. He flipped her around and smashed deep. Her forehead scrunched, and that facial expression returned: mouth to the side, eyebrow slanted.

A memory glimmered from my senior year in Arizona . . . her face screwing up the same way from tequila . . . entering a dark room on a dare with her . . . barely sliding inside . . . knocks on the door.

I clicked away from the video and onto the girl's bio. Her hair in the pictures was shorter than I remembered. And lighter. But her porn star name confirmed she was my first. She had borrowed mine, calling herself "Alexxx."

I'd heard of people finding old flames on dating pages but never on a porn site. She became yet another reason why I was glad to leave behind trashy Arizona.

My boys had never met her, but they would laugh their asses off at the bar. My exciting discovery wouldn't let me chill out, and I had to do something to relax.

I counted backward from ten. My breath shifted, deep and steady, and my chub went away. By the count of one, my eyelids sank.

. . .

. . .

. . .

DON'T HIT DADDY

Even when I slept, I couldn't rest. Had this dream I was flat on my back in the Grand Canyon. Sun flooded the valley, but I was unable to shade my eyes because I lost my arms. They had snagged on the ravine brush, shedding similar to snakeskin. I crackled like a dry leaf when I rolled over.

At ground level, a mural of stick figures held my attention: boys hunting birds, cavemen sparking fires, women roasting meals. My vision climbed the orange walls, and halfway to the top, the hieroglyphics evolved into graffiti. I squinted at the indecipherable style, waiting for clarity until moments from my life—birth prints, recent credit card balance—sharpened into view. The curved embankment was a panoramic museum of my existence.

Shadows crowded the basin. A swarm of stealth bombers covered the sky. The angular frames of each plane interlocked, clicking into one another like racing tracks. They sealed together to comprise a domed roof.

Somehow, I knew the Grand Canyon had swapped into a stadium. The rough terrain under my waist smoothened into cement. The centralized air dropped the temperature. I was cold but couldn't wrap myself up.

The exit signs at every tunnel clicked on like streetlamps, and my vision scaled the embankment. I noticed the boulders along the rim were substituted by a banner of screens. A transformer kicked in, and a jumble of large televisions, computer monitors, and cell phones flickered.

The screens produced an electronic mosaic. The featured woman donned a red catsuit and black leather jacket. The diamonds on her dangling belt buckle sprinkled the audience with pins of light. I stared into the rafters. The hidden crowd grumbled, whispering my name. I had done something wrong but didn't know what.

Her raised arms hushed the crowd.

"A question," she began. "What do the appendix and the wisdom tooth share in common?"

Spotlights scanned the arena. The stands were packed. Each section was occupied by delegates who had rolled to the convention on similar wheels: a cluster of bicyclists in spandex, a clique of manbun hoverboarders, a batch of daisy-duke rollerbladers. There were many more groups in attendance. Steampunkers on high wheelers. Boomers in wheelchairs.

"The answer is," she said, "both are unnecessary. Hence, I ask you, what do we do with what is unnecessary?"

She paused before answering, "We destroy them!"

The masses roared with approval. The spike in decibels pushed down on my chest.

The speaker's face was blurry, her skin gray. But from the clothes and the bougie tone, it could only be one person.

"We gather here to end an era," Miss Jackson said. "Should you be the lucky winner to hunt Alex down, I implore you to hit him. Repeatedly. Ruthlessly. But darlings, please save the last bit for me. Why, I have a surprise for you. And for him. Now look, who votes with me in correcting history?"

Arms shot up around the amphitheater.

"The future is ours!" she yelled.

Fists pumped, hands slapped. In addition, shoebox covers were hoisted with scalpels raised. A club of miming unicyclists juggled lighters.

"Before you light him up," Miss Jackson said, "I have a final question."

She paused.

"Can you hit him?"

The chamber cheered.

"Can you *hit* him?"

The yelling amplified.

Her arms lifted toward the eaves: "Can—you—hit—hi-i-im?"

The stadium exploded.

Every group charged in my direction, and the ground rumbled under my back. My body felt dense. I wanted to escape but couldn't run. Couldn't move.

I thought I was rocking in place in order to stand, but then I realized the only things moving were my shifting eyeballs.

Tens of thousands of wheels spun closer.

"Get that punk," they hollered.

A chick on a Razor snatched me.

"Cut that punk," her girlfriends screeched.

They sped away from the other packs and pinned me

into their shoebox cover. Fingers massaged my backside to bunch the skin in a straight line. Long nails cut me at the crown, pinching downward.

"Hurry up with that blunt," a girl said.

I realized they had been calling me a blunt the whole time, not a punk.

She seized me, nibbling my spine, perforating each node. She split me in half and all my tobacco fell out, my innards smelling like purple grape.

Two politicians on Segways bulldozed through the Razor group. The party representatives stretched my body from opposite corners, claiming eminent domain. They screamed into the lapel mics attached to their suits, arguing with bold claims as to which side could roll me the fattest.

I was quickly dying.

My eyes seeped when their voices began to trail off. At least, if anything, I found solace that I had given Shawna to the world. They continued to tug on my splayed, empty body. What a regretful image to complete the exhibition of my life.

My energy flatlined.

But on my final exhale, I was shocked back to life.

Nimble fingers packed my body with premium cannabis. My laceration was sutured, and I took in a full breath. The emergency transplant was performed by the miming unicyclists. They wore berets, striped shirts, and suspenders. But they were engaged in a silent argument of their own. They pointed at each other, shrugging shoulders in return. They lost their lighters.

The BMX gang skidded to a stop.

Black teardrops appeared on the mimes. Their white gloves outlined a house that they attempted to crowd into. Nonetheless, hiding from the bullies was not possible, and I was peacefully transferred through an imaginary window.

The bike leader wrapped his mouth around my noggin. His peach fuzz tickled my brow, making my forehead itchy. My toes went aflame, and my ten little piggies became kindling. His deep inhalation smogged my brain. I was burning hot, and my lobes were crackling. Once he finished the lion's share, I was ashy up to the waist.

He passed me to the next teen who wore braces. His humid breath leavened the corn nuts trapped in his wires. Slobber entered my nostrils. But he wasn't paying attention and mistimed the turning bank, crashing. I flew from his hand and slid down the slope.

The momentum rolled me in the direction of an exit. I sped toward safety, but I heard a motorcycle rev from inside the tunnel. Emerging from the passageway was Mom's husband. I couldn't halt my progress. He pinched my neck to pick me up.

"Little bastard," he said into my face. "Forget your mom and Miss Jackson—I'm ending you."

He relit me, and my chest sizzled worse than it had from my kid asthma. He woulda vacuumed a lungful, but I was clogged by bready corn nuts

"You're not burning right," he said. "You've never been good for anything."

He popped a wheely and flicked me away.

I fluttered into soft hands. The eyes staring down at me were as tender as a mother regarding her child. From her hair to her lips, the collarbones to the earlobes, she didn't need to say a word. I knew who she was. Shawna was twenty-one, the age when I had her, and breathtaking. My baby will save me, I thought.

Cameras were trained on Shawna. She sat on a stool at the edge of a stage. A guitar strap hung around her neck. Her name flashed on the screens for another sold out concert.

"Did I ever tell you about my dad?" she said after a sip of water. "Or, so-called-dad. I was barely a year old when he took off."

"No, baby!" I screamed. "I never left you."

"As you all know," she said, "I got my start as a childhood talk show host. Sometimes, I watch the reruns, and I'll see an older man sitting by himself in the audience. Salt-and-pepper hair, pudgy waist. And I'll wonder if that's him."

"Look down," I rasped with charred vocal cords. "Daddy's right here!"

"Other times, I'll see the same type at the mall. I want to go up and say, 'Are you my dad?'" She strummed the guitar. "But in that moment, when I'm about to tap on a stranger's shoulder, I know it's not him."

"I never went anywhere. Believe me!"

"And then I'll watch him for a moment go into a shoe store, but I end up getting bummed for the day. Isn't that ridiculous?"

"Please Shawna. Listen!"

"I just don't get it," she said. "How do you ghost your own daughter? I will never forgive him for making things hard on mom."

"If I had legs," I said hoarsely, "I'd walk to the other side of the world for you."

"And that's how I came up with this song."

Shawna plucked a few notes. The audience clapped.

"Yeah, you know this one. Sing along with me. But first things first, let me finish this off."

To the cheers of the crowd, Shawna brought me to her mouth. I could see her teeth.

The audience chanted for her to hit me, hit me, hit me.

The stadium lights reflected on her glossy lips. The stickiness smothered me.

With the last of my voice, I whispered, "No, baby. No. You're the only girl I ever loved!"

The fight in me, every morsel of strength, was gone. I couldn't push Shawna away. Her lungs drew me in, toking me down to the soul.

My jaw disintegrated.

. . .

. . .

. . .

SMOKY KARAOKE

The tablet rang and I lunged awake. Gasping. Snippets of the dream replayed: running, hiding, a mouth. The images faded.

Kaleb's name flashed on the Caller ID. I dreaded to answer. The week had caught up to me. But if I never picked up, they'd shake my window bars later and bang on the doors to rattle the shoebox with a private earthquake. There was no hiding, anyway. Those fools knew about the doo doo key.

Maybe they would accept a rain check. I answered with the hope of feeling him out.

"Yo-yo-yo," I said.

"You sleeping?"

I cleared my throat. "What's good?"

In the background, I heard the popping of paintball guns. Erick and Jerry were with him. Before our night began, they were playing a few matches. I hadn't spent a Saturday there in ages. If push came to shove, my electric gun could sell for a few hundred.

K asked if Shawna was with her mom.

"Dude," I said. "Drama."

"With Ang?"

"Nope."

"With her mom?"

"Yup-yup-yup."

I knew what was coming up next.

"Miss Jackson can get it," K said. "I'd tap that ass, son. *Bop bop bop*."

"You know that booty's fake, right?"

"Watch the news," he replied. "Fake Booties Matter, too."

"So dumb."

"She started the movement."

"Better use three condoms," I said. "Contamination."

"I'd tap that in a Hazmat."

"Go for it," I said. "She'll wrap your dick with the hiv."

"Like a bacon-wrapped hotdog?"

"LA style."

"You gonna miss me?"

"Like a third nut."

"Pour some out for the homies then," he said. "Speaking of dranks, what's birthday boy sipping on tonight?"

"To be honest, I'm kinda broke, and, uhh, I'm kinda—"

"Don't sweat it," Kaleb finished. "We got you! Put

on a costume."

"I don't care about that this year."

"We bought pinstripe vests and trench coats. Crime bosses!"

"I just wanna get fucking wasted."

"Alright then. But just don't wear those same sweats and blue slippers."

I checked the time when he hung up. I hadn't slept three hours in the middle of the day since high school. The clocks would go back the next morning to offer a bonus hour; yet, the following days would be dark until St. Patrick's. Supposedly, the vaccine would be available by then. Worrying about mask filters and Covid farts would be a thing of the past. In 2020, I hadn't heard any live music, let alone a deejay in a club.

I crossed my ankles, and my thighs pinched my sack. Adjusting myself, I noticed the fitted bottom sheet stained with carrot mush. Pizza oil streaked the cotton with a sheen similar to jizz.

I would play them the Alexxx video during appetizers. If timed just right, their drinks would Bellagio across the table. When we're fifty and sitting at a card table behind a giraffe jumper (whose kid will have a kid first?), we'll reminisce about the good old days. A memory such as that will always be worth recapping.

But first, a lot needed to get done.

I grabbed the broom.

The window was blue with the coming night. Across the alley, the white trucks were gone. Construction had ended for the weekend.

I was still working on my place, vacuuming under the futon. The back was raised, sheets stripped. The sweeper skirted my half of the mantle, and the final task was to fold the clothes dumped on the merch coffee table.

While they had been drying, I watched a YouTube video on how to start a dropshipping company. The same book was mentioned in three separate videos. I searched for a free version online but wound up buying a used copy for ninety-nine cents. If I started selling goods with that approach, my place wouldn't resemble a storage unit.

A knock at the door surprised me. The Mormons and Jehovah's Witnesses had stopped distributing their pamphlets months ago. The jiggling chain lock cut my breath short. Dorian's door had rattled the same way.

The vacuum droned while I locked the handle upright. The click was as dangerous sounding as a 9 mm cocked behind a peephole. I squeezed my keys. The teeth bit into my fingers, and the ache returned to my left hand. I lowered onto the ground and crawled toward the backdoor. But then a familiar voice said my name.

"Uhh, yeah?"

"It's Carlo."

What the hell does my landlord want? I wondered. I swear to God if he is about to kick up my rent because of Dorian.

I clicked off the sweeper.

"Be right there."

Carlo owned the building but resembled a laborer from Home Depot. Scuffed boots, dusty jeans. He and his wife owned two more properties, fixing everything themselves. His V-neck sagged into a U.

He complimented the clean smell and asked how I was doing.

"Good," I said. "Good."

"Wait," he said, noticing the boxes. "Don't tell me you're moving."

"That's my inventory."

"Skateboard stuff, right?"

"Uh-huh."

Through a paper mask, he said, "About last night."

"I didn't mean for it to go there."

"Good riddance," he said. "They've been squatting for months. I'm sorry you went through that."

"Naw," I said. "It's all good."

Carlo adjusted his pants. All gut, no butt. He passed an envelope.

"This is from me and the wife. She wanted to be here, but she's having a flare up."

"What's this?"

"Honestly, it's not much for saving that mom and her daughter, but you did a good deed."

A pair of gift cards were inside. Fifty bucks each!

I barely caught the rest of his words—security doors would be installed, something else about homeless sneaking into the laundry nook—because I was busy planning what to buy. The Visa card would cover groceries before the EBT hit, and the Target card would buy that Rams hitch cover my uncle mentioned. I thanked Carlo again before he left and then I folded towels, stunned.

The refrigerator rattled while I mentally separated the clothes. Bibs, onesies, socks, tank tops. More than anything else, I owned more black t-shirts from bars that Dad got for free.

That dark heap brought Allison to mind. The long sweep of her dress, the lines on her cheek from sleeping on the hijab. While other neighbors had pointed their cell phones at me, Allison protected my daughter. Those old hands rubbed her shoulders while my own were cuffed behind my back. Indents on my hand remained from the keys. I realized I'd forgotten to thank her again.

On both cards, the "To" and the "From" sections were empty. With my Sharpie reserved for outgoing packages, I wrote Allison's name on the Target card. I almost signed my name, but she mighta rejected the gift due to modesty. I wrote *Shawna*.

I poked my head into the hallway. Carlo had left.

I rushed over to Allison's unit. Behind the door, airy flutes and wavy twangs played. Something told me not to knock, so I jammed the gift under her door. The card cover got a little scrunched.

I headed back to my place and hopped in the shower. It never felt better. My skin doesn't usually get burned, but my forehead felt the water spray more than usual. I also noticed a faint outline along my arms and neck where my tank top had been. A part of me wanted to curl up in the tub and let the water pound my body until I awoke with wrinkled fingertips.

The crust on my lip had worked itself off and didn't look so bad afterward. Same was true for the shrinking bruise on my jaw. While shaving, I got hungry again and decided to leave the clothes unfolded. I loaded the Visa to my Uber app and put TGI Fridays as my destination.

I threw on a black t-shirt, but since we were celebrating my born day, I busted out the iron and slid on a white, short-sleeved shirt. The driver arrived and pointed to his face. I ran back inside for a mask.

Underneath the restaurant's red striped awning, families waited on benches. Kids were costumed although they couldn't trick or treat.

Through the large window, social distancing measures were apparent. Tables had been removed. Every other booth was skipped. A birthday dessert was delivered, but none of the servers sang or tied on balloons.

The hostess estimated a two-hour wait. I hit up my dad since he knows local nightspots better than Yelp. He texted a link to a nearby Irish pub that he had worked on not too long ago. A throwback neighborhood joint, he noted, where the drinks were insanely cheap. Even more insane were the nightly riots he reported witnessing in Portland. But he was making money hand over fist consulting for outdoor bar setups.

The next Uber dropped me off beside a green bike rack shaped into a shamrock. Rugby banners stretched across the building's paneling, and neon signs flashed in the high, square windows.

I waited in line. The neighboring laundromat pumped out heat, hardening the stench of old milk and grease traps from the alley. My mask softened the taste, and beneath the full moon, I pinned the location to the group chat.

The bouncer guarding the divider belt sat on a barrel. Every few minutes, his fro would poke through the entrance. The sound of a good time would escape. Then, he'd close the door and chew gum, working the stick like a cube of raw steak. He wore a face shield and watched every car pass by.

A middle-aged couple left the establishment. He clicked a hand counter.

"Busy night," I said.

He stared forward, chewing.

I spoke up behind my mask.

"Heard you," he said. "It's Halloween on karaoke night."

Karaoke? I thought.

The setup had to be outside since indoor karaoke was banned.

He pushed my license through a machine and blacklighted both sides. His thick fingers tortured my plastic ID. Bending it, flicking it, picking it.

My chest tightened.

"Don't destroy my shit," I wanted to say.

But his crooked knuckles were not caused by skateboarding, and his cauliflower ears were not from cooking.

"Celebrating my birthday late this year," I said.

He unhooked the divider.

"Get a blow job tonight," he said.

"Alright," I said, unsure if I heard him right.

The door closed behind me. I stopped in confusion. Social distancing was thrown to the wind. Standing room only. Perimeter chairs filled. Every pool table taken. Dart games with waiting challengers.

I looked up to the TVs, wondering if I had missed a major announcement. Perhaps, the vaccine was released early. Across the screens, the Dodgers'

World Series win from Tuesday was being replayed. The vibe inside that bar felt the same as any October night from years past.

By the time I made it four-deep, I removed my mask like most of the crowd. The wooden taps were brand new, each handle polished. No chips, no scratches. My sights shifted to the shelves. More options than inside a dispensary were lit-up: green whiskeys, blue gins, yellow tequilas, clear vodkas. Courvoisier was the top-shelf cognac, and I knew my order: a double, neat. I'd start with that, then end with it later in the shoebox.

The bartender poured in a rhythm, slapping down change, jumping to the next patron.

Ten minutes passed and my legs ached from standing. I rubbed my thigh and remembered my day: Shawna's bubbly wake up call, that drive-thru prick calling me a fruity nutjob, Miss Jackson's eyelashes hitting the cement.

Two chicks were ahead of me. One wore devil horns. The other wore a halo. They asked the bartender the dumbest questions: "What tastes good? *Hee hee*. Does that have white rum or brown rum? *Tee hee hee*. Is it happy hour?"

He handed over the drink menu and mentioned his favorites. They giggled at the specialty names while their fingers underlined the ingredients (cham-bord, ver-mouth, per-sim-mon.)

His head shook, and my hand shot up.

Moments later, he returned with my order. But a round ball of ice sat inside the snifter. He noticed his mistake.

"No worries," I said.

"Hold on," he said, and poured a neat glass on the side.

The chicks were engrossed by the plastic menu and didn't see him slide to another couple. They also didn't take notice of the guys who had left before them. The crowd shifted and with my drinks held high, I turned sideways to stretch past the girls.

Even though my face was calm, I was excited to sit at a bar top again. Two empty mugs sat on crumpled dollar bills. I placed their glassware onto a Ketel One drip mat.

The lacquered wood held a shiny finish. Red lights squiggled in a puddle of suds. I dried my area with cocktail napkins and grabbed a coaster for my drink. A leprechaun was imprinted on the ice. I sent a pic to the homies and asked where they were at.

I swiveled around and checked out the costumes. Through the action, I saw the decor on the brick walls. They had the usual mirrored beer signs and pictures of boxers from the black and white days. The name of the bar, Hooligan's, was smack dab in the middle. Old English font, extra-large lettering. That had my dad's signature all over it.

Some time ago, he was flown to a bar and grill

in Pittsburgh. He got tore up from free drinks, and his memory lapsed, forgetting where he was. Ever since then, distinguishable signage is a must.

The karaoke host tightened the mic stand. A tall girl asked questions, and he pointed her to the song folder. Her Superwoman costume reminded me of my daughter's pajamas.

Before turning back around, I was tripping on the difference between this place and the empty bar at TGI Fridays. The stools there had been replaced by tall planters. Their busser probably continued sanitizing each plastic plant. Meanwhile, the barback at Hooligan's dumped fresh ice into the well.

I dipped my pinky into my drink. The fluid tingled the roof of my mouth. The warmth was similar to Shawna's gums, and I wondered which tooth would come next.

Grandpa had about just as many teeth before he died. He'd watch baseball from his recliner and dip tortilla chips into a crock pot of chili. During money games, he'd sip on "grandpa juice." I wasn't much bigger than Shawna when I imitated his infamous *ahhh* with my milk.

In the overhead screens, the Dodgers threw the winning pitch. Gloves flew into the air. Players dove into a dogpile. Man, what my grandpa woulda done to watch that moment with his great-granddaughter on his lap. Before dumping back the shot, I thought, To you, G-Pops.

Black hair filled my peripheral vision. A girl asked if anybody had the seat. My hand jabbed toward the stool.

Superwoman slid on, and we bumped knees. She looked around, then pressed the button on her vape. She started to cough, her eyes wet, and she appeared lost, trapped in an undercurrent.

I didn't know her, so I didn't feel comfortable slapping her on the back to help her cough.

"Customer needs help," I said to the bartender at the far end. "Yo, bartender!"

Her lungs barked. She appeared on the cusp of getting sick.

I leaned over the dark walnut and pulled a glass from the chiller. The soda gun had more buttons than a remote control, but I figured out the water.

"Here," I said. "Take this."

She drank half the glass.

"Saliva," she explained. "Wrong tube."

"I understand."

The bartender ran over.

"What the hell are you doing?"

"Rick," she said, "I was about to die."

Her hand hovered over her chest, and a big cough came out.

"Aw shit," he said, with a softened tone. "I thought you were a customer."

"I'm a customer now," she said. "If this is our final karaoke, I had to be here."

They touched cheeks over the napkin-straw caddy.

"I'd never disrespect your bar," I said.

He accepted my apology and said to her, "Your hair's dark."

"I showered."

"Time for a Winky?"

"You read my mind."

I'd never heard of a Winky. It was probably a house specialty, some foo-foo drink garnished with fruits and plastic monkeys.

She napkinned her cheeks.

"Feeling better?" I said.

"Oh my God, yeah."

Superwoman had a heart-shaped nose stud and a gold star bandana. Her natural eyebrows were sleek.

"You probably thought I had Covid," she said.

"I already had it."

Her eyes widened.

"Me, too," she said. "All I had was a headache. Which I thought was my period."

"Same," I said. "Except for the period part."

"Well, I hope not."

"You never know. This is Long Beach," I said. "Besides that first big headache, I had back spasms. But it was over in two days."

"Our owner is so over it," Superwoman said. "We're closing for the election in case of more looting. They trashed this place during the riots.

Our mayor forgot to put on his big boy pants that day."

"Supposedly, the governor might shut down the state for Thanksgiving."

"You're joking!"

"Serious."

"And to think, we've been doing this since March. Our grand opening was right after Valentine's Day."

"Ouch. That blows."

"Then, it was like, 'Let's flatten the curve for a couple of weeks.' But do these two weeks ever end?"

The bartender delivered a light beer. She relayed to him what the owner had explained to the morning crew. That the books couldn't survive another shutdown. That she was opening to full capacity and lifting mask rules until they forced her to shut down. She'd had it with the changing rules and was moving back to Florida where her other bar was pulling in more dough than ever.

Superwoman raised her glass and toasted, "To unemployment, bitches."

"Exactly," replied the bartender.

Her tongue smacked. That reaction meant she had swigged a tangy cider.

Superwoman let out a soft side burp.

"I'm Stacey," she said.

An hour later, my grandpa juice was gone. The

ice ball had shrunken in the snifter, but I was buzzing something nice.

The fellas texted they were running behind. A group of fifteen-year-olds had challenged them to lightning rounds on the speedball course.

"Hurry," I typed, although I knew they were chronically late.

If it was possible, they would still be chilling in the womb, snacking on Doritos inside their moms' bellies, smearing orange fingertips on uterine linings.

The night was too young to be wasted already, so I checked out the taps. I didn't see the Winky handle. Maybe it was a bottled selection.

"How's that beer?" I asked Stacey.

Before she could answer, my dad's microbrew lingo flowed from my lips, beer vocabulary pouring like a bottomless pitcher.

"Does it have earthy hops," I said, "or a cinnamon sheen? Is the finish decadent or crisp?"

Honestly, beer discussions bore me. Only thing lamer are chicks who gab about their first tattoo for hours.

For some reason, and I don't get why, but girls dig guys who can describe tastes. Yet the explanation of IPA varietals spilling from my mouth surprised my own ears. I was talking about some golden-caramel-note, roasted-pine-bouquet, dancing-amber-hue type stuff.

By the time I tapped out, Stacey's face had

glazed over. Her cheeks were flushed from two beers. She was a lightweight.

"This Winky here," her answer began. "This beer right here is pure magic."

She dipped a straw, trapping in the fluid with her finger. The pink on her nails was jagged. She twirled the black plastic around the rim.

"Hocus pocus," she said. "Try this."

My mouth parted for the sample.

"Wait," she said.

Stacey released the beer down her throat. She poured the remainder of her pint over my ice.

"I want you to get the full, um, array."

She waved over the bartender.

"Rick, he's trying a Winky."

A towel was tucked into his pants. He dried his hands.

"My all-time favorite," he said with a grin. "Tell me what you think."

The pressure was on. No matter how the beer tasted, my review would be positive.

"Cheers," I said.

Stacey was right. The palette was simple: a blonde ale with a balance of strawberry notes. But when I swallowed, the magic kicked in. Pure black magic.

My shoulder quaked from the lace of hard alcohol. I almost spit into the snifter.

"What is that?" I said.

They chuckled, and the bartender poured a new glass for Stacey. The mug was filled with three-quarters beer. When Stacey confirmed the manager was not around, he reached into the well to dump in vodka.

"You want one?" he asked with a wink. "Same price as a beer."

"Going out of business sale," Stacey added.

Our seats swiveled toward each other. She admitted to a few extra Covid pounds, but that sort of thing never bothered me. Some guys can estimate cup sizes with numbers, but I only know three categories: little, regular, and big. Hers were somewhere between regular and big.

We exchanged stories about all the craziness, reflecting on how nothing made sense. "Outdoor seating" inside plastic-bubbled patios. The "political progress" that stalled the second stimulus check. A "deadly virus" that barely killed anyone our age.

"And how much Costco toilet paper," I said, "does one asshole need?"

"Right?" she said, touching my shoulder.

Stacey was bartending through school to become a child psychologist. After Long Beach State, she wanted to return to Minnesota for grad school, but their governor was crazier than the rest combined.

I usually don't slide Shawna into conversation, but I felt comfortable enough to show her a picture.

When I told Stacey about Miss Jackson, she said,

"We just read about that! They call that a form of 'maternal gatekeeping.'"

"She did stop me at the gate."

Because Stacey would be out of work soon, I was about to tell her she could donate her plasma for money. It woulda been kinda cool to meet up there and make cash while connected to neighboring plasma machines. But the lights in the bar dimmed, and the karaoke host began to sing. Between verses, he crooned directions, holding the clipboard above his head to entice volunteers.

The first guy bombed but received an ovation.

"I can't see from here," Stacey said.

To face the singers, her stool scooted between my legs. Every once in a while, she would lean back and belt out choruses with the crowd. Her hair dried to brunette and smelled good.

My hand brushed the side of her jeans. She didn't mind. Neither did she mind when my palm rested on her thigh, fingers tapping to the beat.

With each Winky, time blinkied.

"Rick," she said, "This Libra here needs a blowjob."

"Say what?" I said.

"You're here for your birthday," she said. "You need a blowjob."

A layered shot appeared: dark bottom, tan middle, whip cream top. That's what the bouncer had mentioned.

"Put your mouth around it," she said. "Don't use your hands."

"Serious?"

"Suck it back, baby."

I searched through the darkness. Thank God my friends weren't there recording my mouth around the glass. I wiped the cream off my lips and thought of the Alexxx video. I would show them, but only if Stacey wasn't around.

She caught the attention of the karaoke host. He reviewed the list and held up four fingers.

"Great," she said. "I have time to smoke a bowl. I hate singing flat."

We went to the patio. The cool air was refreshing after the packed bar. In the back corner, past the cigarette smokers, was a shed.

"Let's be quick," she said.

Corrugated plastic topped its weather-beaten sides. The holes in the green roof filtered light from the streetlamp. We posted up on empty kegs.

The wheel on her lighter spun, illuminating her double chambered pipe. The alley stench returned to my nose until the hit brightened her face.

"Kush," I guessed.

"Very good," she croaked through a cloud.

When she finished, muscle memory took over my hands. The butt of the lighter patted down each bowl, and I flicked the flame. The fire volleyed, cherrying both sides. I flattened the tank over the chambers and missed that burn in my lungs.

"Pro," she said.

"I'm good," I told her after the second hit.

"We have a minute," she responded.

With tarped chairs and broken tables around us, we kissed in the darkened shed. I heard the thrum of the patio. Bottles dropped in the trash, cornhole cushions landed, guys howled.

My high lips felt like I was simultaneously kissing her mouth, cheek, and eye. I slowed down. Our tongues glided, the timing just right.

Stacey held my hand through the crammed patio. Her head was as close to the market lights as my own. The strings shone brighter, as if each bulb was dipped in shellac. Conversation snippets entered my ears more precisely than if delivered through headphones. The weed had me feeling so good, I coulda stopped to chat with everyone and befriended the entire patio.

"I have to pee," Stacey said.

I waited for her at the end of the hallway.

The fellas texted that they would be there after showering. They were starving and wanted the menu forwarded.

When I told them I met a chick who had friends, a parade of orgy memes came through. I fired back a few of my own, but then I wondered how long I had been standing there. Maybe she had walked past me already.

My stomach grumbled at the bar top. I searched around for a QR code. The bartender was slammed, so I couldn't catch him for a food menu.

Rather than endure a singer with a squeaky voice, I decided to search for Stacey. I went by the darts and the TouchTunes machine. I hoped she hadn't left. Maybe she went outside to look for me.

I found her back at the bar top. Our Winkies were refreshed.

"Where's your friends?" Stacey asked.

"They're coming," I said. "I'm hungry."

"By law now, we have to have food," she said. "But we loopholed that by serving Cup Noodles."

"You mean Cup O'Noodles?"

"That's what I thought!" she said. "But honest to God, it's Cup . . . Noodles."

"Shut up. It's Cup O'Noodles."

"Look at the box!"

Beneath the register sat a giant pack the size of a hamper. I read the packaging and reread it, blinking. No lie, it said "Cup" followed by "Noodles." At that moment, I don't think I've ever felt as high. It's like I fell backward into the "O" that I thought was in Cup O'Noodles, but I could never return since it never existed.

That light stuff in my stomach wouldn't cut it. After her turn, I'd ask if she wanted to eat somewhere. If the fellas showed up after—oh, well. They made me wait, so I could make them wait. It was my damn birthday.

I drank the Winky like water. The harsh taste had disappeared, and I tipped back the pint for the last drop. Neon lights from the bar swirled inside the empty glass. I set it down and suddenly we were kissing again. Her tongue transferred her gum to my mouth.

"Next on the list," the karaoke host said, "we have our very own. Put your hands together for the sultry, sexy, Stacey."

She pulled on me to go with her.

"Way high," I said.

"C'mon."

"Not my thing."

High as balls, Stacey went to the karaoke table. She stared at the monitor and gripped the microphone, pinky lifted. The words appeared, but she knew the lyrics by heart. Stacey sang off-key, at times almost screaming. The host turned down the vocals.

During the second verse, her voice dried out. She coughed. Lines scrolled down the screen.

I didn't want people to think airborne droplets were being dispersed, so I delivered her drink. While taking appreciative sips, she passed the mic. Her hand spun for me to catch up to the bouncing ball. We sang from the same microphone.

"Ladies and gentlemen," the host announced, "our first duet of the night!"

The room exceeding capacity clapped for us. But my focus switched to Stacey's gum. Musta been a fresh stick of cinnamon. The sharp juices slid into my stomach, and Shawna's gums from the previous night popped into my head. They had been red as grenadine.

My eyes bounced around the audience. The bar was packed with faces, some with masks, some with Halloween makeup. The angel girl and the devil girl stared. A heavy draft of patio smoke hit my face, and I became queasy. Hot.

The conversation with the cops in the hallway came to mind. Thoughts of my parole officer triggered a reminder that I had a piss test on Tuesday.

My thoughts spun. What if the THC wasn't out of my system? What if I lost my daughter over a few tokes?

The whole crowd felt like they were staring and judging. I drowned in their body heat.

Stacey's eyes raised.

"You okay?" she whispered. "You're all sweaty."

The words on the screen fell. I couldn't read anymore.

"Not . . . feel good," I said, voice trailing off.

"What did you say, Al?"

My eyes were closed. I felt her embrace. She asked if I needed air. I nodded.

Just then, the layers of the Blowjob, mixed with

acidic cinnamon, came up my throat. I attempted to break away from Stacey, but my mouth spewed, catching the S on her chest. I dropped to my knees and hunched over the floor. The force of each hurl clacked my balls against my collarbone. Clumps heavier than wet dog hair drenched the carpet.

"Yo!" I heard. "Is that Al?"

"C'mon, dawg."

"My dude!"

Kaleb, Erick, and Jerry surrounded me. They wore Goodwill trench coats and pinstripe pants. Whichever one helped me up had a red garter belt over his white, long-sleeved shirt. His spats were clean, unlike my short-sleeved shirt.

The last thing I remember from the pub was the karaoke screen. That finishing *Ooh* went on forever.

Before we hit the cold outside, my perceptions arrived in flashes. A flash of Kaleb's car. A flash of his backseat.

When K asked what happened, I mumbled, "Got too drunk . . . got too high."

They laughed while the air slapped my cheeks. More streetlights zipped past in flashes.

Jerry turned around from the passenger side.

"How'd you get kicked out of your own birthday?" he said. "I thought you stopped smoking."

"Winky," I explained.

Erick beside me asked, "What?"

"Win-kee."

"He's about to knock out," Erick said. "Hey, Alex!"

But the car flashed away and everything disappeared-*disa-disa-disa* . . . *dis* . . . *ap* . . . *peared.*

ESCAPE TO BUTTERFLY AVE

My vision throbbed the next morning. The clean laundry on the boxes pulsed with my heartbeat. The folded towels jittered, the garments emitted ghosts. From the ground, a phantom husk hovered over the bedsheet.

I was naked on my futon, but at least the fellas had tried to cover me. But they didn't know the trick with the tablet. As soon as I double wrapped the wire, messages chimed. Most names were unfamiliar. Some unlisted.

I musta done something real dumb since video files were attached. I tried to rundown what happened . . . smoking in the shack . . . throwing up on stage . . . hearing my friends' laughter . . . blacking out.

My jaw was tight. I forced my mouth open. The connecter joints popped, ringing my skull. Nausea overpowered me, and I rumbled to the toilet, dropped to my knees, but nothing came out. I shut my eyes and rested my head on the rim of the tub.

Smooth, cool. I woulda fallen asleep there had the mildew stink not been replaced with vomit.

I wiped around my mouth. I sniffed my fingers then blew hard out each nostril. The stench remained. My eyes parted, and the drain appeared clogged by oatmeal. The bloated pieces were strips of chewed tortilla. I gripped the toilet seat, hunching. There was no telling how painful the hangover would be that day. My stomach ached from the dry heaves.

I swallowed two Advils from the cabinet with hopes they would stay down. In the mirror, the tired eyes of an old man with more years than my dad glared back. Sweat kinked my curls, and my tight skin was dark from a day of boarding. The tan shaded my yellow jaw and the sun exposure widened my freckles. When I finally hit my uncle's age, they will bake into chocolate chips like his.

My neighbor's radio played through the ceiling. Before the pandemic began, he was living the hermit life already. Weirdo spent his days in the bathroom listening to AM, constantly turning the dial for traffic updates. The announcer reported a shutdown on the 710/405 connector. CHP on scene. Overturned big rig. Jaws of life.

My head pounded when I started to think about it. If I were that person smashed in the commuter car, the reporter wouldn't quit his job. There'd always be more traffic jams. More Sig-Alerts. More celebrity gossip. More stock reports.

Besides a few internet posts, my death would not trend. Not even in my own city. Marches would not be organized. Murals would not be dedicated. After the presidential election in a few days, I'd be forgotten. My baby would be too young to hold a single memory of me.

I returned to the room. More plinks from my phone sounded. Before piecing the night back together, I needed to smell fresh air.

In order to be covered up in the alley, I snatched clothes from the heap: red basketball shorts, yellow shirt. I stepped into my blue sandals and slid on my green sunglasses from the mantle. Rocking that many colors, I coulda scribbled *Skittles* on my forehead as my costume the night before.

Daylight savings gave me an extra hour to sleep, but the sun was mad that I gave half the day to the previous night. Sunshine pierced my cheap lenses, and I lost my footing. My hip caught the porch railing, and my hands skidded on the cement.

This, I thought, is my life.

I crawled to the bottom step and picked at the gravel. I spit on my burning palms, wiping the pitted skin. I readjusted my shades, but the sunshine was punishing. I needed the world to stop moving, stop spinning.

Even though it was bright outside, my day was done. I had no energy. My best bet was to rub one out and sleep it off. But that plan meant getting up from where I'd fallen, and I had yet to catch my breath.

The shadow from the condo next door sliced across the alley, cutting my stoop in half. I leaned against the shady side and considered brewing coffee. Knowing the first cup might come right back out of me, I rested my elbows on the high step. I didn't know why smoking weed had freaked me out so badly the previous night. Green tea and niacin would erase the weed from my system.

The ocean breeze ruffled the palm trees. My choppy breath settled while the sun covered the steps. There was no escaping the morning shine. I closed my eyes, basking. The heat on my skin felt fine. Not too weak, not too strong.

The nausea eased, but messages continued to chime. I knew I had to face whatever happened the previous night, yet at least I wasn't in jail. I probably needed to apologize to a few people. Most definitely to that girl. I couldn't recall if I got her number.

Down the alley, between a fence and a phone pole, an adult tricycle was parked. Large back wheels. Chopper-type handlebars. Tourists rent those lowriders on the beach path. But the lights strung along the tarp were fading in and out, dying. Either it was stolen, or the rider had veered off course, never to come back.

I sat up taller. No cars or people had passed by.

I'm not sure what it was, but something told me to look it over. Like a tweeker hunting for spare parts, I kicked the tires and checked the chain. Seemed tight enough.

I used the doo-doo key to lock the shoebox and decided to go for a ride. I wiped the fire soot off the orange padded seat. The sign in the alley posted a ten-mile speed limit.

I was eye level with car rims spinning down Fourth Street. Being that low to the ground reminded me of my knee boarding days. So that I wouldn't get run over and broadcasted through my neighbor's radio, I snaked up a driveway.

My knees were flared, legs pumping like wings. While recalling my Big Wheel, I slammed on the brakes, then reviewed the skid marks. I smelled the rubber, and the thought of catching a DUI on a trike brought on a chuckle. But considering my weekend, it wouldn't have surprised me.

The cross street had a coned bike lane. I gained momentum down a small hill, and my old stomping grounds came up quickly. From a distance, the faces at the skate park looked unfamiliar. To save my own from embarrassment, I bent a corner down Peacock Route.

A gust blew the orange sky inland. A crew of green parrots, unfazed by the Santa Anas, flocked toward the bluff. Zigzagging in unison, their chirps cyphered a rhythm that rose and fell, and I felt my head nodding to the natural beat they bumped.

The underside of a car scraped a dip, and my attention returned to the skate course. While passing God's Fart, I remembered coming down from the times I had gotten high on that couch. Before landing back to reality, my brain would settle, attention sharpened upon everything in the moment.

The green parrots glided toward the beach, and a similar sense of calm overcame me. My eyes fluttered from here to there, my focus tightened on Peacock Route, while the busy atmosphere braided in with my breath, interconnecting my surroundings.

The incense for sale on the corner table cast a ribbon of smoke up to the streetlight, prompting a young couple with a double stroller to cross the intersection that was striped with Pride colors. A tiny sandal sailed from the swings. It slid across a sidewalk decorated with chalk drawings that had been smeared by the shuffling feet of football fans in matching jerseys. They crowded around a cell phone, cheering. Their scream startled a soccer player who sliced a kick out of bounds, and the ball bounced across the street to smack a yard gate that was crowned with iron, curlicue hearts, protecting a Black Lives Matter stake in the grass.

I passed the cafe. Mimosas and Bloody Marys clinked over breakfast plates. But I musta still been the drunkest in the LBC. I was confused yet calm, forgetting to pedal while immersed in the scenery shifting as fluidly as a video game with no glitch.

My environment blended like pieces to a puzzle, nothing out of place, nothing out of order. Not even the cackling hacky sackers near the water fountain, nor the tinkling dominos shuffled beside the auditorium. The elote man stopped ringing his bell to hand over a steaming piece of corn doused with red pepper to a teenager in a wheelchair walking a schnauzer that was sniffing a bush. At the other end of the shrubbery, a graduate in cap and gown posed beneath a buzzing drone. Everything remained in flow, making sense at a whole new level.

"Oh, hey," a voice said, breaking me from my zone. "It was you!"

A woman rode at my side. The silhouette on the bike was lean. From my seated vantage, I saw yoga pants. They were printed with elephants hooked by trunks and tails.

"Yeah-yeah-yeah," I said, recognizing the gap in her teeth. "You helped me out yesterday."

The Veggie Hutt chick smiled. Half of her face was painted for Día de los Muertos.

"Thanks again," I said.

"My roommate showed me the video this morning, and I was like, 'That's him. That's the guy with the big car I told you about.'"

"Huh?"

She answered, "You were really—"

"What video?"

We crossed Ocean Boulevard to the grassy bluff overlooking the water. Hundreds of people—every shade, size, age—were on mats, socially distancing to stretch before yoga.

"Umm," I said, looking up, "I think you got me confused."

"It's you," she said, smiling with that slight gap. Her teeth appeared brushed, unlike my own.

"You have, like, ten thousand views."

"What?"

"Check your phone. It's everywhere."

"Mine's charging."

We stopped on the sidewalk. Fingers pointed my way from the crowd. How many people had seen it? No wonder my cell was blowing up.

"I'm kinda embarrassed," I said. "Last night was my—"

"Embarrassed?" she said. "That was incredible!"

I thought of the Buddha her business card and took a deep breath.

"Hold up," I said. "I'm super confused, Veronica."

"Brianna."

"Ah, man," I apologized. "I—I don't . . ."

Nothing made sense. My friends and I can be assholes, but a vomit video would be something we'd share amongst ourselves, not posted for the entire world to view . . . unless . . . it was pure comedy. Maybe they had caught me at the perfect angle when I splashed that girl's boobs. Or maybe it was something that happened on the ride home. More than likely, someone at the bar had downloaded the video.

"I'm Al," I said, lumbering out of the lowrider. My hands stung a little from the fall. I motioned toward her pocket. "You cool showing me?"

Brianna's phone was in perfect condition. Her protective case was the expensive kind.

"Starts out blurry," Bree said. The painted bone structure of her face was on my side. "I can't believe you haven't seen this."

The title to the video was "Fight Last Night!!" The thumbnail previewed two fuzzy forms in a tussle. Did I sock the bouncer? I squeezed my hands and patted my face. Neither caused me to wince.

Brianna tapped the screen, and a warning appeared: possible inappropriate material. I braced myself and leaned closer, covering my mouth to feign concentration, but really, it was to hide my breath. Of all times to bump into her.

The video posted by the handle "HelloKittyKim" started out brightly. The shaky camera traveled beneath ceiling fixtures. The covers to the long, fluorescent bulbs were cracked.

I didn't remember the bar lights ever coming on, so the footage musta began after I had hurled. But then again, there was a lot I didn't remember.

The cellphone turned a corner. When the movement stopped, the walls were undecorated. Bare. Instead of the pub, I saw the grungy walls of my apartment building.

The two grainy figures standing toe-to-toe came into focus. The video paused with an arrow pointing to Dorian as "The Wifebeater."

HelloKittyKim inserted an explanation page: "This guy was beating up his wife. You can hear his daughter crying. Then my other neighbor showed up . . . lmfao."

My heart sped after the fight part when the cops entered the front door. Thankfully, they did not come through the side and view me from behind with the knife. From that angle, it woulda been a wrap for me.

The video skipped to me handcuffed. It was strange to see myself staring at the ground and shaking my head. Out of the shot were the captured flies in the webs, but I remember thinking that my life was over then. Once I was released, I looked toward the cell phone and rubbed my wrists.

I figured out who HelloKittyKim was. She was the high school girl who lived in the unit with her mom. They own *Hello Kitty* everything, including a welcome mat with the eyes rubbed off.

"I'm—I don't believe it."

"The views are growing," she said.

"This is wild."

"A GoFund me has been set up for the daughter."

"Good for her."

"You're a hero," Brianna said. "I would be honored for you to join me today."

"For what?"

Her hand opened toward the large group.

"It's been a long time," I said.

"Please," she said, patting her bike rack. "I always pack an extra. By the way, where's your baby?"

"With her mom."

"Oh, okay."

My head spun from the shock. Before I knew it, I had parked the lowrider and laid out the mat, leaving space for hers.

"Great," Bree said. "Let's talk later."

She coursed through the crowd. She probably had friends who had arrived earlier. Brianna leaned her bike against a tree, removed her helmet, and reached the center of the large gathering. She removed her shoes and waved to everyone. She unzipped a microphone from her backpack.

"Good morning," she said, voice booming though a handheld speaker. "How do we do, yogis?"

She repeated answers shouted her way.

"'We do the best we can while we still can do.'" She giggled. "I like that one."

I realized they had been pointing at her earlier.

Brianna started the yoga session, wandering through the lanes of bodies in her elephant-printed pants. I followed my neighbors' movements. Arms needled through thighs. Torsos torqued over hips.

She returned to her mat for downward dog, and I remembered when I had thought of her in a similar position. Yesterday felt like a million years ago. She reminded us to breathe, but certain poses throbbed my temple.

"Fists pinned to our Earth," Bree instructed, "and kick both legs to the sky."

Everybody reminded me of donkeys. My morning high from the ride had worn off, and the headstand took me out of the game. I considered returning her mat so that I could check my calls. I wanted to scroll through the online comments to see the public response. But I didn't wanna be rude and interrupt her practice.

I opted for Yogi's Choice. At the outset, she announced that we could switch to any practice tailored to our individual needs. My choice was to lay on my back. To appear more yoga-like, I connected the bottom of my feet.

My mind gave in to the coastal sounds. Kids and waves. Pelicans and wind. In the distance, a drum circle patterned a tempo, as calming as CBD for the brain. Their synced hands slapped a rhythm that patted me to sleep.

I woke up toward the end of the session. My

hangover hadn't ended, but the nap softened my headache. People had eased into a seated posture, wrists flipped to the sun. I joined with a yawn. I've done yoga a few times. The leader delivers a calm pep talk that ends with "Namaste."

Brianna surveyed the crowd. We caught eyes for a moment. I looked down and played with the grass.

"I stand up here each Sunday," she began into the mic, "telling you to be at peace with your life. To accept yourself, your body, your circumstances. But there are times when my message has not been authentic, and I leave here feeling like a fake, a failure. For not practicing what I preach. For not being true with you or myself. Well, friends, this will not be one of those days."

I plucked a few blades, lining them side by side. They reminded me of a joint, so I snuck a pretend toke. Then I rolled the grass to pack an imaginary bong. Complete with water gurgling sounds, I faked a hard rip. Next to my knee, a ladybug stopped on a tiny white flower. I placed the ball of grass on Bree's mat. The blades accordioned, crinkling into little escalators. I bridged a piece onto the petals, and the red beetle with no spots went down to the mat. When it flew away, my invented high was intact, and I was ready to hear what Bree had to say.

"As you know, I am extreme about everything,"

she said, turning between sentences. I saw the unpainted side of her face beneath her dreads.

"I always thought that if I pushed myself to the extreme, until it hurt, I could conquer anything. When I was younger, that mindset always paid off: first in my family to serve in the Marines; first from my NorCal town to earn an MBA.

"I kept going, always moving forward, never stopping. I started my own store, purchased my own home, and bought a big sedan because a baby would not be safe on a superbike. But a year ago, after losing my house in the divorce, everything shut down, everything stopped. And, no, I'm not referring to the Coronavirus."

Brianna pulled off her shirt. A black sports bra hovered above her butterfly tattoo.

"For eight months, I carried my little butterfly. Every day, for eight months, her flapping wings blessed my tummy. But those eight months ended." Her arms crossed her midsection. "Worst day ever."

I stopped messing with the grass and looked around. She had everyone's attention.

Brianna clicked off the mic and set down the speaker. Just as she had done at Meat Shake, she pounded her hip. The blows to her pants landed directly to the crown of a printed elephant. The vicious banging struck with enough force to stun a real one into submission.

"I blamed myself for being too busy," she yelled

across the bluff. "For wearing too many hats at once. For not slowing down. The doctor, she told me . . . she said, 'Brianna, these things just happen.' If that's true, then why doesn't this pain in my heart 'just happen' to go away? Please, doctor, by all means, suggest more options that 'just happen' to work for others but never me. I've tried everything! Therapy, prayer, prescriptions. Group meetings, exercise, sounds baths. Yet every day, I wake up angry."

My throat knuckled. The word "angry" brought Miss Jackson to mind. I forced her out of my head, focusing my attention on Brianna who rocked, heel-to-toe. She squeezed her bottom lip and stared toward the beach. The Queen Mary sounded. Noon. Never had so many container ships been anchored in the water. There were cruise ships that hadn't voyaged in months.

"And yesterday," Bree screamed. "Yesterday, I honestly thought I was going to kill somebody! This man, who already irked me, was being rude to his customer. And his customer had this absolutely beautiful baby in the backseat. Seriously, I couldn't pull my eyes away from her precious face."

Bree ran her tongue against her teeth. She swiped her face but didn't peer my way. To recompose, she hit her hip once more and retrieved the microphone.

"Because for a moment, in that split second, I thought she was *my* butterfly. I mean, she looked exactly like my dreams. Oh, the dreams I have about her! The best is when she allows me to touch her face. Skin so soft, my fingers disappeared into her cheeks the last time she visited me."

Brianna rubbed below her belly button. She shared that the tattoo artist had blended the ashes into the ink, camouflaging the scar with the butterfly's spine.

Rows ahead of me, an older woman sobbed. Her husband scooted off his mat. Gripped her shoulder. He whispered, and her face met in his chest. They were not the only ones crying. A surfer with his shirt off cleared his throat but couldn't shunt the tears.

My molars pinched my gums. I imagined the tables turned—tiny coffin, small plot, headstone with one date. I felt insignificant, a maggot, a gnat, to think I had problems. Gravity squeezed me, and I rushed into Child's Pose. My back quaked over the mat. I cupped my hot face, and the mat felt dangerous as a raft drifting past the oil-drilling islands visible from the Long Beach coastline. Because of everything that had happened, I was scared to get torn apart by whatever else might await me that day. The ambush of misery seemed never ending.

But out of all the events from my crazy weekend, my mind returned to Shawna bucking in my arms Friday night. When things are the hardest with my daughter, I realized how lucky I am to have those struggles, proven by the little tooth in her smile.

"Everything went red on me, yesterday," Brianna said, "I swear, I was a breath away from seriously hurting him. How insane would that have been if you found out your yoga teacher was being held up on charges?"

She laughed.

Giggles followed from the group.

My breath softened, and I regained control. I peered between my ankles. No one seemed to notice I'd had a moment.

"There's enough ugliness in the world," Bree added. "During this bizarre era, when folks have been horrendous, I've witnessed cars in downtown honking for hospital workers, kennels emptied by adopters, teddy bears in windows for the children—I could go on and on. But that baby gave me hope yesterday. And her father, who I learned more about, he reaffirmed that the good fight is still happening. I know things won't ever be the same, but we will get through these days together."

I unfolded and rolled onto my bottom. I held my feet and let my legs flap. I wanted my tattoos to be filled in with bright colors like Bree's.

She set the mic down one last time.

"And so I leave you with this," she yelled, raising her arms. "Remember to look for each other's wings today. Some people show their feathers at every turn, always willing to provide a helping hand. Then, there are those who leave you feeling exposed. But maybe their past defeathered them, and what remains are shoulder nubs that barely wiggle.

"In these closing moments, I want you to conjure someone like that, someone who *does not* give you hope. I want you to take this time to find their wings. This can be scary and uncomfortable. But for sixty seconds, push yourself and lift yourself higher today."

A meditation gong played off Brianna's phone. If it was any other day, I woulda heard the reverberations through the microphone and thought it was corny. But Brianna, who gave me the mat I laid on, who didn't single me out during her story, had bared her soul with no filter.

I held my breath, feeling the pressure build. Automatically, Miss Jackson came to mind. With her beak-thin nose and chicken shit attitude.

Where did her wings go?

She gave them to Mister Jackson who plucked them clean. Then he cooped her up alone in a crappy neighborhood to raise two daughters. Faster than devouring a Superbowl appetizer, he jackknifed those two little bones, scraped the meat off her wings, and squeezed her heart in his teeth. No wonder she flashes her breasts and thighs at every turn. That's all she has left.

The gong hit once more. The hollow tone curled,

and that was the moment I realized it.

I lost.

No matter how many times my head spun the situation like a Rubik's Cube, no matter how badly I wanted Shawna to live under a single roof, she would be raised in two homes. Angela's eyes at the gate had proven it.

And if I wasn't careful, Miss J would manipulate the divide she designed until Shawna would be wedged from my life. I had to pull my head out of the clouds and face the hard facts. Miss Jackson was a man-hater who would never acknowledge my efforts. In her chicken brain, since her husband ditched her, and the same thing happened to her oldest daughter, Miss J wanted to protect her youngest from being pigeon-holed next.

As much as I hated to admit it, Miss Jackson did love Shawna. She would do anything to shelter her from pain, even if that meant removing me from the picture. But if I did leave, Miss Jackson would pick up my wings from the ground, dust off the feathers, and glue them on as her own.

Sometimes, you have to give in to win. For the next seventeen years, I would focus on Shawna and not worry about her mom's side.

Seventeen years . . . seventeen years.

The numbers felt equivalent to a prison sentence. But when that time is up, and Shawna reaches adulthood, Miss Jackson's selfishness—it's inevitable—will leave a sour taste in her mouth. My daughter will be proud that her daddy never tried to leave. The payback would not be instant, but I figured out my escape plan. Like Angela said, "This is the flow," and on my tombstone, there won't be engravings of any shoulda, coulda, wouldas for nothing.

A refurbished Mustang rolled up to the traffic light. Waxed and pristine, the classic car was the kind my dad loved. With its windows down and the system up, I heard a female voice sing a remake of his favorite *Sublime* song: "Summertime . . . and the living's easy."

I half expected him there, but my sights landed on the older couple. They leaned against each other. They were nodding, not to the beat, but to the song in life they had produced together, a song all their own that could never be replicated. I didn't know their story, but I could tell that they had made it through harder times than a lockdown. One day, I would have that. I'd have a woman who had my back. No matter what.

Cymbals rang from Bree's fingers.

"Now is the time to fly," she said. "Fly beyond yourself. Fly beyond what you think is possible. With that, we end today's practice. Namaste."

I repeated the term with the crowd, but the word passing through my lips felt soft. In a weak way. I considered whispering, "Namaste, bitches," since it rolled off the tongue better. But that was too gruff for the moment.

I sat tall, maintaining steady breath. My arms straightened down to the ground, fully exposing the two red dots in the crooks of my arms from donating plasma. My fingers dug into the ground. After the weekend I'd had, I was thankful to be alive on this Earth, not dead inside it.

Brianna tapped her finger cymbals three times. The high pitch quiver reminded me of Allison's music. I then knew what to say: "Alhamdulilah."

What that word meant exactly, I didn't know. But to me, it meant I loved Shawna and nothing else mattered. In those fleeting seconds, I felt at peace, knowing that no matter what happened to me on this planet, I did my part to keep the world twisting, never to skip a beat, forever destined to keep spinning on *and on and on and on and on . . .*

Crate Digging

"Shoebox Fever" based on **"Good Daddy" by Atmosphere** from the album *Sad Clown Bad Spring #12* released by Rhymesayers Entertainment (2008)

"Cuffed Wings" based on **"Dorian" by Brother Ali** from the album *Shadows on the Sun* released by Rhymesayers Entertainment (2003)

"Baby Pearly" based on **"Lacville '79" by Devin the Dude** from the album *Just Tryin' ta Live* released by Rap-A-Lot (2002)

"Meat Bree" based on **"Drive-Thru" by Ugly Duckling** from the album *Taste the Secret* released by Emperor Norton (2003)

"Spray Painted Ice Cream" based on **"Kick, Push" by Lupe Fiasco** from the album *Food & Liquor* released by 1st & 15th (2006)

"You're Sorry, Miss Jackson" based on **"Ms. Jackson" by Outkast** from the album *Stankonia* released by LaFace (2000)

"Grandma Timeout" based on **"Bonnie and Clyde '97"
by Eminem** from the album *The Slim Shady LP* released
by Aftermath (1999)

"Huevos de Tapatio" based on **"Gotta Get Some
Lovin" by Too Short** from the album *Get In Where You
Fit In* released by Jive records (1993)

"Don't Hit Daddy" based on **"Can't Wake Up (I'm a
Blunt)" by KRS-ONE** from the album *Return of the
Boom Bap* released by Jive Records (1993)

"Smoky Karaoke" based on **"Kinda High, Kinda
Drunk" by Coolio** from the album *Gangsta's Paradise*
released by Tommy Boy (1995)

"Escape to Butterfly Ave" based on **"Sunshine" by
Atmosphere** from the album *Sad Clown Bad Year #12*
released by Rhymesayers Entertainment (2008)

Reading Group Guide

In this novel comprised of chapters grounded in Hip Hop songs, Max Evans explores the courage of a young dad who raises a teething daughter amidst the stress of the Covid pandemic. With his skateboarding days in the past, Al must deftly maneuver the obstacles hindering his paternal involvement: a healthcare industry that patronizes fathers, a legal system that defaults to mothers, and a materialistic society that relegates men as monetary providers, not emotional supporters, to their children. In his quest to evolve for the betterment of Shawna, Al's insecurities are exposed during this transformative —and often comedic—weekend.

Max Evans readjusts the perceptions of fatherhood with *Escape to Butterfly Ave* while simultaneously revolutionizing fiction by mixing a minimalist approach with an urban flair for an adult contemporary audience.

Discussion Qs

---

1) What Covid Era memories did the novel spark for you?

2) This novel is basically a mixtape of songs. From all the songs that you personally know, what songs would you link together to create a story?

3) Is the author of *Escape to Butterfly Ave* biting the creativity of the songwriters?

4) To encompass his multi-racial composition, Al describes himself as "Long Beach mutt." Do racial characterizations filter your readings?

5) Have you ever seen or met someone reminiscent of Al?

6) Do Al's thoughts of killing Miss Jackson indicate a severe personality disorder or merely encompass a daydream?

7) What is the biggest surprise in this novel?

8) What does Shawna's tooth symbolize?

9) How many hours span the plot's timeline?

10) Would a third-person perspective alter the text?

11) How is tone manipulated to provide the material a special flavor?

12) Correlate Al with the evolution of the cycle of a butterfly: Caterpillar (Hungry Crawling Phase), Pupa (Stagnant Transition Phase), and Adult (Free Flying Phase).

13) Al despises Miss Jackson's materialism, but how are his ideals similar?

14) What does Al's schedule look like the following week?

15) Writing is a form of acting but with words; however, does a writer's physical appearance affect your reading experience?

16) What does Al's "shoebox" studio symbolize?

17) How financially secure do you project Al will be when Shawna enters high school?

18) What event or action could change Miss Jackson's opinion of the main character?

19) Does the slang hinder or enhance your reading?

20) What characterizations are revealed from the settings?

Convo with Max Evans

What inspired you to write this novel?

I zone out a lot. Made-up events unfold in my mind for no reason. I think it has to do with being an only child because you become normalized to letting your mind wander freely. In the studio of my mind, I've dunked on Kobe (RIP), bought a beachfront home in cash, and been a guest on *The Arsenio Hall Show.*

In the summer of 2016, I had been invited to join Hip Hop podcasts to discuss my first book, *Where's Pops?* I had also recently read the evolutionary predecessor to this novel called *Lit Riffs*, published by MTV Books. It was a collection of short stories written by different authors based on their favorite songs.

So, I'm zoning out hard in my apartment, imagining myself in the audience of a Hip Hop symposium. Slug, the emcee for *Atmosphere*, was on stage taking questions. When I reached the microphone, I said, "You're the greatest storyteller in Hip Hop. Why don't you create an album that's a novel of songs that connect to each other from start to finish?" The crowd ooh'd and ahh'd at this prospect. (Again, in reality, I was probably staring at a drape, picking my nose, entranced by my imagination.) However, Slug, who I've never met before, can be a smart ass. He threw back at me,

"Why don't you combine a bunch of songs to make a novel?" Bam—my mind took off with this unique concept for a novel.

What was the process to write this novel?

It took three years to get started. At that time, I had accepted a full-time position to teach English at a dysfunctional college which wound up obliterating my soul. To begin, the department chair was sleeping with a fellow probationary faculty member, yet he threw her under the bus once their dalliance was discovered. It didn't help to have three presidents in four years; I had zero confidence in that institution. Not only that, but the *woke* movement on the part of some of the professors there equated to sheer racism. That backward perspective was epitomized by a *TMZ* report featuring one of their instructors who called a Latino police officer a Mexican racist and claimed he was threatening to murder her with her son in the car. All that just because she had believed that would get her out of a simple driving ticket.

Once I figured out my escape plan from Los Angeles Southwest College, I made a list of Hip Hop songs that contained a story—a beginning, a middle, an end—and played narrative Tetris to see what would fit together. After that, I wrote chapter summaries and knew I was on to something unique.

But early on, I hit a harsh reality regarding my audience. I shared my outline with close friends who I thought would love the concept since we used to carry record crates into Hip Hop clubs that we hosted. I was super hyped to ask if they would review it and give me some feedback; however, none of them ever hit me back with ideas. In fact, about a third of the printed outlines were left to die on the table.

The harsh reality I came to is that, in general, those who love Hip Hop don't read novels, and those who read novels don't love Hip Hop. Nevertheless, I persisted from the perspective that if I enjoy both sides of this chasm, then I will find the millions of weirdoes like me who love Hip Hop and books equally. *Field of Dreams*-style.

Originally, my goal was to replicate each song as close to the original text as possible. However, the chapter based on OutKast's "Miss Jackson" threw me for a loop because a clear-cut story is not told—it's more of a rant against a mother-in-law. Then, I really caught fits with Eminem's "'97 Bonnie and Clyde" because of its intense, murderous details. Some beta readers viewed Al as demented and untrustworthy thereafter. I realized I had to use each song for what it contributed to the overall story, even if that meant cutting out chunks from the original texts.

Bonus info: the novel's original title had been a Beastie Boys homage, "Here's a Little Story I'd Like to Tell."

With Hip Hop as a major influence, and taking a que from the movie Brown Sugar, I'll be the corny interviewer to ask, "When did you fall in love with Hip Hop?"

Ha ha! "Bro-o-o-o-wn Sugar." Mos Def killed that theme track.

Alright, so really, the first song I clearly remember… it's kind of funny. Summer of 1987, I was about ten, when I heard "Wipeout." Even if you're into Hip Hop, you probably don't remember that song. The Fat Boys had collaborated with the The Beach Boys to reprise the original 60s hit by The Surfaris.

"Wipeout" is super corny. The crossover track details how The Fat Boys went on vacation to a California beach after three years of touring. But in comparison to the other songs that played on KIIS-FM, that track landed differently in my ears. Through the radio speakers, the syncopated word delivery was addicting, not to mention the emcees were funny. I heard my first turntable scratch in that song, and The Fat Boys were doing this weird thing with their mouths called beatboxing. In the video, they partied amidst a mix of people on a packed seashore, so The Fat Boys were inclusive before "inclusive" was included in our vocabulary.

That's when I turned the dial to search for more of the same sound. Turning the radio knob became a gateway to Public Enemy, D-Nice, and Gang Starr. I was blessed to go to high school during the Golden Era of Hip Hop, the mid-90s. My friends from then, who I hang with to this day, were equally in tune with the culture. We listened to Hip Hop while playing basketball at parks where you entered the court by peeling up a lower corner section of its chain link fence. We listened to Hip Hop while scouting the malls to scope out the newest Nikes. Honestly, without Hip Hop and basketball in my life during that time, I might have killed myself.

But the biggest thing I gained from Hip Hop is the artistic criterion of "fresh." In other words, to create something original at a high skill level which is fully satisfying. That's why I find the book publishing world baffling. The original meaning of "novel" means when something is new, innovative, and unique; however, most novels are not *novel* because their approaches are old, stale, and overused. Genre writers literally have checklists of elements to include and are scared to do anything fresh. Even if *Escape to Butterfly Ave* is not your cup of tea, when compared to the other cookie-cutter novels you read this year, you certainly will not forget this one.

What was the biggest challenge in writing this "fresh" text?

Going into the first chapter, I felt rusty. Over a year had passed since I approved the galley copy for my first book. Secondly, my natural talent in creative writing is with the short story form, so the idea of writing a novel always felt foreign and unnecessary to try. On top of that, I knew that writing a novel takes a long, long, long time. Along my writing path, I've met writers who worked on their first novels for more than two decades.

Most people give it up. That's why I gave months to the outline so that I could keep my eye on the prize. I knew the novel had the thrust to lift off the ground based on the first chapter winning the Donald Drury award.

What did you learn the most while writing this novel?

When I hits walls, I don't freak out as much. Whether it be from determining how to smoothen out a confusing plot point or actively listening to a challenging chapter review, my internal state is much calmer than the past. Partially, this has to do with age. My brain spun too quickly when I was younger. Easily thrown off. I appreciate the RPM it currently runs at because my coasting speed is efficient, but I can still hit the gas pedal when needed. Also, I've faced so many writing challenges that I rarely overheat. But every once in a while, I get a boulder in my stomach, and I rush to the toilet from the nervous squirts, still tapping away on my computer while seated. Personally, if you never get a similar reaction from writing, do you even write?

Why is your hometown a mainstay in your fiction?

Because Long Beach has all the flavor. You can travel the world in a day in this city. We differentiate ourselves from LA is because we've germinated a concentrated culture not diluted by hours of traffic and glitzy Hollywood glamour. In fact, Long Beach doesn't drive to LA unless it's for work or to take out-of-town visitors. Their traffic is a formidable wall. In the other direction, the OC has a different wall—financial. From houses to a haircut, everything costs more there, so we stay put and appreciate our climate voted the best in the nation. Because of the great weather, different elements bump into each other at a faster rate here. People of all feathers flock together at backyard barbeques and house parties resulting in a ton of mixed babies. In my own house while growing up, we were a blended family. My half-Salvadoran mom speaks fluent Spanish, and she married my dad who is black when I was a baby.

Because of my city's diversity, we hold a long history of forging our own paths. For example, Billy Jean King who championed gender equality proved it by defeating a male player on national TV. When our school system believed it was more equitable (and safe) for students to wear a uniform, suddenly cities across the nation followed our lead. And when it comes to music, not only do we have Snoop, but we had Bradley Nowell from *Sublime*. He is the greatest artist ever from the 562 to wrap all the cultural flavors of our city into a burrito. All these greats have influenced me to do just do me. If you're from Long Beach, you just can't do things the way everyone else does.

You mentioned your dad who raised you and who you characterized in your first book as "Pops." But I understand that your biological father was a well-known writer.

Yeah, he did a lot in the Western genre. Published over 30 books. Turned some into movies and a TV series, *The*

Rounders. He was voted into the Western Writers Hall of Fame alongside fellow inductee, Clint Eastwood. Technically, I'm his Junior since we share the same first and last names, and I must explain we're not the same person when I visit older, indie bookstores.

But I didn't know him, never met him. That was by his choice. In college, I initiated a letter correspondence which was done in secret. He didn't want his wife to know about me, so I sent the letters to his friend's house. We had the same handwriting which was weird, and we both disliked academia's ignorant hand in literature. But then, he basically rejected me again and stopped writing back. He was a selfish asshole, and I'm sure the other children he had out of wedlock would agree.

He died in 2020, and it was such a relief because now I can feel comfortable saying these things. But, on the flipside, I would not have been such a dedicated father — working multiple jobs while getting through school before entering my career — without that experience. I also can't foresee the topic of fathering ever missing from my fiction.

Negative to positive.

If academia's "ignorant hand in fiction" is not your audience, then who is your book for?

My target audience cyphers at the corner of Big L and Junot Diaz illuminated beneath the lamp post of Raymond Carver minimalism.

In other words, my adult contemporary audience celebrates a minimalist approach with an urban flair. These readers are not impressed by the current market of extreme fantasy and filler pages equivalent to empty calories in a processed meal. They hunger to witness soul on the page via the setbacks and triumphs of a realistic character whose parenting struggles are universal. They have a bend toward Hip Hop culture but are fulfilled by the skillful, fresh narratives.

What is your upcoming writing project?

I'm sticking with Remix Fiction but flipping back to my strength: short stories. The working title is *B-Side Champions* and features adaptations of Hip Hop cuts again, but they will remain independent of each other. My writing muscles were bolstered from composing a novel. That burgeoning strength will allow me to flex the most memorable short stories of my career.

Beyond that, I'm outlining a larger novel called *The Five-Man Weave*. The story follows a group of friends whose lives are blended for decades by the game of basketball. I envision that story more as a movie, so I'm learning about how to write screenplays. But for now, making social media videos satisfies my creative side.

Acknowledgements

Thank you to my parents for believing in the kid even as the hairs on his chinny chin-chin sprout more gray each year.

Love to my son for marking in his spot in the world but never forgetting where he came from.

Special recognition to Darren Smoley at LBCC, our city's best instructor of creative writing.

Heartfelt spotlight on my beta readers who gave insight where too much salt had been added and where sections needed more sweetening.

Salute to my editor, Christy Krumm Richard, who smoothed out the sharp ends and went above and beyond the nuts and bolts of editing for the sake of the narrative.

Praises to Katarina Naskovski from Serbia for creating a stunning cover.

Shout out to my friends and family who supported me through this journey, even if we haven't spoken in years, or even if I had to bark at you sometimes to prove the love was real.

And lastly, to my city, Long Beach, where I was born, raised, educated, and—hopefully—will die. You marinated me with the flavor, consciousness, and determination to manifest my existence, helping me to discover my true self with every word in these pages.

Previous Work by Max Evans

Where's Pops? is the first short story collection to focus exclusively on fathers as central characters—the good, the bad, and the rest in-between. These central characters reflect the diverse population of Long Beach and regardless of where these men land on the spectrum of fatherhood, they each face relatable challenges: relationship tests, financial hardships, and cooking dinner on time.

All sales of *Where's Pops?* continue to fund a scholarship I created for deserving fathers attending local community colleges.

The MVP Award (Most Valuable Pops) is distributed annually. Check my social media for more details.

SOCIAL MEDIA:

LONG BEACH WRITER

9 7 9 8 9 8 6 3 2 7 1 0 5